THE PIG AT 37 PINECREST DRIVE

WESTMINSTER PRESS BOOKS
BY
SUSAN FLEMING

The Pig at 37 Pinecrest Drive

Trapped on the Golden Flyer

The Pig
at
37 Pinecrest Drive

BY
SUSAN FLEMING

ILLUSTRATED BY
BETH AND JOE KRUSH

THE WESTMINSTER PRESS
PHILADELPHIA

Book Design by Dorothy Alden Smith

First edition

PUBLISHED BY THE WESTMINSTER PRESS ®
PHILADELPHIA, PENNSYLVANIA
PRINTED IN THE UNITED STATES OF AMERICA

9 8 7 6 5 4 3 2 1

Library of Congress Cataloging in Publication Data

Fleming, Susan, 1932–
   The pig at 37 Pinecrest Drive.

   SUMMARY: His mother's latest "educational expe-rience" gives Terry the notoriety he thought he wanted, in addition to a quick lesson in politics and handy knowledge about pigs.
   [1.   Mothers and sons—Fiction.   2.   Pigs—Fiction.   3.   Humorous stories]   I.   Krush, Beth.
II.   Krush, Joe.   III.   Title.
PZ7.F623Pi   [Fic]   80-22391
ISBN   0–664–32676–5

*For Amy
and the children on Morton Street*

CONTENTS

Continued

THE PIG AT 37 PINECREST DRIVE

1. "Is This National Pig Week?"

Mom sure threw me a curve. I didn't suspect a thing, though, as I ran up Pinecrest Drive that Monday afternoon in early April.

The air was warm, the trees were beginning to leaf out, the lawns were getting green, and I was hoping that one of the AAA Little League captains this spring would be me, N.V.N. Terry Blodgett, a Not Very Noticeable guy at Longfellow School. If I were a captain, I'd stand out for a change. I didn't realize then, as I stopped in the middle of the sidewalk and wound up for an imaginary pitch, that standing out isn't always so great.

Kaiser, Miss Dowd's German shepherd, who lives next door on the left side of our house, barked at me.

"Oh, keep quiet, you big brute," I yelled at him as

I opened the gate into our backyard.

My mother was sitting on the back steps holding my baby brother, Clarence Matthew, trying to get him to drink juice out of a cup. That was normal. But there was another baby in the yard—a baby pig!

I felt like a tire with a slow leak. This had to be another of Mom's "educational experiences." Mom used to be a teacher—she has never recovered. Is she content to let us learn things on our own? Oh no. She sets up situations to "enlarge our awareness."

Learning is fun, but I like to learn things that interest *me*. Do you think my mother would arrange an interview with a major-league ballplayer or take me to a Red Sox game in Fenway Park? Not a chance.

Instead, she'll shove me into a car at 5:00 A.M. and drive fifty miles to catch one glimpse of some rare purple-breasted, cross-billed, speckle-throated nuthatch on its way south.

"You've got to broaden your interests, Terry," she says. Well, I'm tired of broadening my interests to match hers.

I took a deep breath and let it out slowly. "Where'd you get the pig?"

"Hi, dear, have a good day?"

"Is this National Pig Week?"

"Not that I know of."

"You're going to enlarge our awareness of the animal kingdom by introducing us to a new animal every week. Next Monday I'll come up the street and find a giraffe with its head hanging over the fence."

"Now, Terry, a pig is not a giraffe."

"No, a pig is not a giraffe. A pig is not a puppy, either, or a hamster or a goldfish. Besides, what's Dad going to say?"

"Pigs are very intelligent. They're so smart they could be trained as seeing-eye animals."

"You're dodging the issue. Dad is not an animal lover."

My sister, Olivia, pushed open the back door and came into the yard, carrying a large yellow plastic pan. She plunked it in front of the pig, who sniffed at it and pushed it with his snout. "We can put the piggy's food in here, Mama. You haven't never used this for a long, long time."

Joel raced in with Twinky Rogers, leaving the gate open. "Mummy, Mummy, Mum, can me and Twinky play over at his house? Please, Mum. We're going to build a fort down in the basement."

"Shut the gate, quick. You two can play in our basement. You know you're not allowed at Twinky's house while his mother is at work."

I tapped Joel on the shoulder and pointed to the pig. "Look."

"Hey, where'd he come from? Mum, Mum, where'd you get the pig?"

"They had extras at the farm, so they gave us one," Olivia explained.

"Do they have extra bunnies? I'd like a bunny," Joel said.

"Don't give her any more ideas," I told him.

Joel disappeared into the house with Twinky.

My mother untied Clarence Matthew's bib, kissed the top of his head, and put him on the ground. "I picked up your grandfather for a drive to Mr. Roscoe's farm and Gramp got to talking about his childhood and the pig he raised—"

"And you thought the four of us would just *love* to raise a pig, too."

"I suppose that's it."

"Now is not the time for the Blodgett family to be taking on new projects. Your campaign is all we can handle."

"He won't be much work."

"Where's he going to live?"

Mom put her hand on my arm. "Look, look! Isn't that adorable the way Clarence Matthew is patting the pig? Let me get my camera quick."

I followed her into the house, put my books down on the kitchen counter, poured myself a tall cold glass of milk from the refrigerator, and grabbed a handful of brownies from the plate on the table. "Dad's not going to like this. You know he doesn't like animals underfoot."

Mother was rummaging in the chest of drawers in the family room just off the kitchen. "The pig won't be in the house. Have you seen my camera? It was here yesterday or the day before."

I went to help her. Maybe if she had a few pictures of the pig, I could persuade her to get rid of it. The camera was hanging from the antlers of the moose

12

head on the wall. Joel must have climbed up on the bookcase to put it there.

"Terry, get between Olivia and Clarence Matthew so I can have you in the picture, too," Mom directed when we were outside again.

"I am not going to have my picture taken with that dumb pig. Take a picture of Olivia and the baby. They like being photographed."

Mom didn't argue. She knelt down on the ground, squinting into the polaroid. "Smile, Olivia. Look toward Clarence Matthew. Move in closer to the pig. That's the way."

My mother is ridiculous the way she wants to put everything on film. If a hydrogen bomb were falling, she'd take a picture of it before she ran for shelter.

"Aren't you afraid that walking ham roast will step on Clarence Matthew's fingers?"

Mom ignored me. "One more. This time, put your arm around the pig, Olivia. Hold it. That's perfect."

I was disgusted. I hadn't received a single intelligent answer to any of my questions. I tried again. "Where is the pig going to live?"

"The toolshed will be a perfect little house for him. I thought you children would help me clear it out."

That made me boil. "This pig wasn't *my* idea. Why should I get stuck with all the dirty work? Joel! Get out here. Fast!"

"Just move the lawn mower and the big bags of peat moss, dear. I'll get the others to do the rest."

"Mom, there are only two weeks before the election. Why can't you wait until *after* you're elected to the School Board to take up pig-raising?"

2. Not Florence

I spent twenty minutes lugging stuff into the garage before I could escape to my room. After dealing with my mother, I actually enjoyed my math homework. Math makes sense. If your answer is right, you can prove it. If it's wrong, you can prove that, too. Nothing vague. It's straight and clear and exact.

By six o'clock, when I heard my father's car crunching over the stones in the driveway and easing into the garage, I'd finished all my work. I wished I could figure out some way to stay in my room until morning. I wasn't looking forward to hearing my parents discuss the pig. But my stomach was growling for supper.

A mouth-watering smell of spaghetti sauce pulled me right into the kitchen. Dad came in through the back door at the same time. He couldn't have seen the pig, because he was smiling.

"You've got one sure vote, Ethel. I want you to know I cast my absentee vote today."

"You mean you're not going to be here for the election, Dad?"

"I'm leaving for Dallas tomorrow morning, Terry, and I won't be back until the day after your mother becomes the new member of Brookside's School Board."

"Dad, we need you to help with Mom's campaign."

"Allied Conglomerates needs me to audit their books. I'm not crazy to go, but that's my job."

Why argue? I'd just get a lecture on duty and needing a roof over our heads. Of course I knew who was going to be asked to do all the things Mom wouldn't have time for. Terrance Woodbury Blodgett, that's who.

Joel jumped up from his seat in front of the TV and ran into the kitchen. "Daddy, Daddy, Dad, Mum brought a pig home from the farm."

Olivia chimed in. "The pig's only a baby. I can wheel her in my doll carriage."

Dad smiled absentmindedly and sat down at the table. "That's nice. When do we eat, Ethel? I'm so hungry I could gobble up the Stock Exchange."

Mom placed a long golden crusty loaf in front of him. "Homemade French bread is tastier." She kissed the bald spot on his head.

We plowed into our supper like fans rushing onto the field after a big game. Dad was heaping his plate with spaghetti for the second time when Olivia broke the silence.

"She must be lonely all by herself."

"Who?"

"The pig. Don't eat everything up, Daddy. She wants a supper, too."

Dad put down his fork. "You mean the pig is real?"

Here comes the explosion, I thought. But before Dad could ask any more questions, Joel said, "I want to name the pig Florence. That's my favorite name."

"Florence is too ordinary. Any pig could be Florence," Olivia told him.

"How many pigs have you known personally that are named Florence?" I asked her.

"The pig is a he," Mom said quietly.

"He's going to be called Cadillac," Olivia told us in a tone that decided the matter.

"Naming your Easter dinner will make it hard to eat, children," Dad said.

"Harvey, the pig is to enjoy, not to eat. We won't keep him forever, and he'll live outside in the toolshed, so you'll hardly know he's around."

"You're missing a good bet, Ethel. Pork on the hoof is cheaper than the sliced and packaged cuts in the supermarket."

Mom didn't say anything. She just smiled and looked at Dad with her morning-glory-blue eyes twinkling.

Dad met her look. "Pigs are to be eaten, dear. And no one could cook a roast suckling pig the way you could. Serve it on the big platter we use on Thanksgiving, put a bright-red apple in its mouth—magnificent. We'll invite your father and all the neighbors to share it."

Olivia slid off her chair and ran out of the room.

"Have you finished your supper, honey?" Mom asked.

Olivia didn't answer. She threw herself down on the sofa in the family room and began to cry.

"What's the matter, 'Livia?" Dad called.

Muffled sobs answered him.

He tried again. "Did you hurt yourself?"

Mom went into the family room and now-now'd and there-there'd. Finally, Olivia allowed herself to be carried back to the kitchen. "Mama, don't let him eat up the baby pig," she blurted out.

Dad adjusted his steel-rimmed glasses. "Excuse me, everyone, for my vulgar thoughts."

"Promise me, Mama, you won't eat up Cadillac."

Dad wiped his mouth on his napkin. "Tell you what, Olivia. We'll give your pig a test and if he passes it, *I'll* promise you he won't be eaten!"

I was suspicious of the look in Dad's eye. "What kind of test are you going to give him?"

"An intelligence test. Remember the three little pigs? We'll bring Cadillac a pile of straw, a pile of sticks, and a pile of bricks. If he knows enough to build himself a house out of bricks, we'll know he's a gifted animal, and his life will be spared."

Mom became angry in a flash. "Harvey, you're

18

mean leading poor Olivia on that way. I don't know what's so terrible about wanting the children to have the experience of knowing and loving a real farm animal."

"I work hard to provide this family with a nice home and I think it's mean to me to turn the backyard into a pigpen." Dad stalked into the family room and buried himself in *The Wall Street Journal.*

3. The Trouble Begins

When the doorbell rang I went to answer it because Mom was putting Clarence Matthew to bed and I knew Dad was in no mood to put his newspaper down.

Mrs. Pomeroy, our neighbor and Mom's campaign manager, had come to go over Mom's schedule for the next two weeks. She made herself at home, spreading out her papers on the kitchen table. "Harvey, do you know if Ethel is free a week from Tuesday? Dorothy Bush says she'll give a coffee then."

"You'll have to ask Ethel," Dad called back without lowering his paper.

Olivia scraped the remains of our supper into the yellow plastic dish. "Mrs. Pomeroy, we have a pet pig named Cadillac."

"Isn't that lovely. I'd like one, too. Tell your mother

I need to see her—I can't stay long."

I went to hurry Mom up. When I came back, Olivia was lugging the pig in through the back door, talking to him as if he were one of her dolls.

I grabbed her arm. "What do you think you're doing?"

She shrugged me away. "I'm feeding a poor, lonesome creature."

"Get him out of here!"

"No."

With Mrs. Pomeroy in the house, I didn't want to use brute force and I didn't want to attract Dad's attention. "Feed him in the laundry room, then get him out."

Cadillac consumed the contents of the plastic dish, his nose twitching as he ate. When he had finished he gave a little deep-throated grunt, which Olivia was sure meant that he wanted more. She raided the refrigerator for leftovers. I helped her, afraid she'd feed Cadillac roast beef. We located some cabbage casserole, stale bread crusts, and a dish of Harvard beets.

Olivia was right about Cadillac wanting more, because he was so excited when we dumped the food into the pan that he tipped it over trying to get at it. A yellowish-greenish, pink-streaked mess spread over the floor.

Cadillac's hoofs clicked on the linoleum as he followed the stream, slurping it up until it ended under the table, where Mrs. Pomeroy's sandaled feet attracted his attention. He moved closer and sniffed at them. Startled, Mrs. Pomeroy jerked her foot and hit Cadillac under the snout. He didn't like that and his mouth closed over her big toe.

She let out a scream that must have split the polar ice cap. It brought my father running. "Jan, Jan, what's wrong?"

Mrs. Pomeroy didn't wait to explain. She was halfway up the sidewalk before Dad reached the front door. "Get rid of that animal," she yelled over her shoulder. "And tell Ethel to call me."

Mom hurried down the hallway from the baby's room. "What happened?"

"She kicked Cadillac and he bit her," Olivia explained.

Dad shut the front door and leaned against it. His face sagged. The clock on the living room mantel struck six times, stopped, then struck once more.

"Ethel, I'm a patient man. When you put the mattress over the cellar stairs so the children could have the fun of sliding down, I never said a word. I can live with the living room being turned into a nursery for a hundred and fifty-three seedling plants and an observatory with a permanently set up telescope. I even bit my tongue when you turned the playroom downstairs into a giant sandbox and bought thirty-six varieties of cactus so that the children could get a feel for the desert. But there are limits to what I can take."

Without raising her voice, Mom said, "Terry, take the pig outside. Harvey, let me bring you a cup of coffee and another slice of pie."

I picked up the pig by his middle. He wasn't a bit

22

cuddly like a puppy. He felt like a chunk of cement.

Dad went to bed early. He looked exhausted. I felt sorry for him—Mom's projects were almost more than I could stand, too.

Our problems with the pig were just beginning. The next morning I woke up to hear Dad bellowing in the kitchen. One look at the floor told me why. Someone, I suspect Olivia, had brought Cadillac into the kitchen for the night. Fortunately, Olivia had had the brains to shut the kitchen door so the pig couldn't get into the rest of the house.

The room smelled terrible because the pig had messed all over the place. He had also figured out how to open the bottom cupboard doors and had rooted out pots, pans, and canned goods. At the moment, Cadillac was amusing himself by rolling a large can of peaches across the floor with his snout.

"I don't work my fingers to the bone for this family for the privilege of getting breakfast in a barnyard. If I've said it once, I've said it a thousand times, *there are no pets allowed in this house,*" Dad roared.

He unscrewed the big glass jar where Mom keeps her homemade doughnuts, pulled out a couple, dropped them on a cookie sheet, and stepped back to open the oven door so he could heat them up. But he tripped over the rolling can of peaches and the doughnuts went flying. Cadillac caught one neatly in his mouth.

Dad's language became unprintable. I lugged Cadillac back to the toolshed, glad to get away from the fireworks.

23

When I came back, Mom was standing at the stove in her plaid bathrobe scrambling eggs.

"I think I'm entitled to a decent, peaceful breakfast without some blasted swine turning this kitchen into a bowling alley," Dad growled.

"Go get shaved, dear," Mom said gently. "Terry and I will have the kitchen cleaned up by the time you're finished."

Why should I clean up after the pig? He wasn't my pet. Why couldn't I be known as Terry Blodgett, Little League captain, instead of the kid who does stupid jobs nobody else wants to do? But I pitched in anyway. It's easier than arguing.

The kitchen was almost back to normal when the Pomeroy kids, Christine and Jimmy, appeared at the back door. Christine is in my class at school and Jimmy is in Joel's. "What are you doing here so early? It's not time to leave for school yet." I was in no mood to be pleasant.

"We want to see the wild animal that bit our mother," Jimmy explained.

Olivia strolled into the kitchen carrying her stuffed monkey. "It's not wild. It's a sweet, lovable little pig."

"You wouldn't think it was so sweet and lovable if you'd had to clean up after it," I yelled at her.

Mom handed Christine and Jimmy each a doughnut and ushered them out the door. "Come back after school this afternoon, children. Mr. Blodgett is in a hurry to catch a plane."

"Where's Cadillac, Mama?"

24

"Outdoors where he belongs, Olivia."

"I woke up and it was so dark and I was afraid he'd catch cold out there all by himself."

"He has his house and we have ours. Don't ever bring him in again, do you understand?"

Dad came into the kitchen carrying his suitcase. "I want everyone to understand something else. That pig will be gone when I get back from Dallas. Gone from the house. Gone from the yard. I will bring home the bacon, but I will not raise it."

I couldn't read Mom's face. She had a calm, sympathetic look that told me nothing. I had an awful feeling that with Dad away she was going to drag her feet about getting rid of Cadillac.

4. "To Mars!"

At school nobody picks me out of the crowd. I don't get terrific marks; I don't get terrible marks. I'm not Mr. Popularity Plus; I'm not Rupert the Repulsive. I'm just a short, quiet kid who does what he's supposed to do.

I get tired of that, if you want to know the truth. I'd like to be recognized. That's probably why I like baseball—it's the one thing I'm good at. I don't think I'm good enough to make Majors. But last year I was given a baseball by the coach for being the most valuable player on our AA team. That's why I think I have a fair shot at becoming an AAA captain.

Soon after Dad left I yanked on my Red Sox cap, grabbed my baseball and glove, and hurried off to school, determined to get in some practice at recess and during lunch hour.

Christine and Jimmy brought the news of our pig to Longfellow School. It spread fast and brought me instant recognition.

As I was passing the office on my way upstairs to class, Mr. Adams, the principal, greeted me with, "Hear you've volunteered to supply the ham for the PTA supper this year, Terry."

Ha, ha, ha. Big joke. He wouldn't be so amused if that four-legged pork chop had spent the night in *his* kitchen.

When I walked into my classroom Toby Phitz squeezed past me and said, "Just because you have a pig at home doesn't mean you can hog the whole doorway, Blodgett."

Mrs. Lambartini, our teacher, made things worse. She knows I hate talking in front of the class, so she is always looking for ways to make me do it. As soon as she heard about our pig, she suggested that I prepare an oral report on hogs and bring Cadillac in to school to show to everyone.

That wasn't really a suggestion—it was a demand. She smiled her hard-candy smile and said, "You can make this a science research project for extra credit. I'll schedule it for Friday afternoon."

A bunch of us played baseball after lunch and I forgot about the pig for a while. Not for long, though. As we were going back into the building I asked Jerry Clarke if he thought the Red Sox would win the pennant this year. He said, "Maybe. Say, does your pig give real piggyback rides?"

When the dismissal bell rang at three, I ducked out the side door to avoid Christine and Jimmy. I knew they'd remember Mom's invitation to come to see the pig after school.

Only a block away from the building they spotted me and ran to catch up. Then Twinky Rogers and Joel appeared, and the Foster twins, Billy and Buddy, who also live on our street.

"We're coming with you. We want to see your pig," Christine announced so the town could hear her.

While we were waiting for the policeman to give us the signal to cross at the intersection of East Street and Washington Avenue, Joel bounded up to a kid I'd never seen before, slung his arm around the kid's shoulder and said, "Want to see our pig, Chucky?"

"Why didn't you tell Mr. Adams to announce it over the loudspeaker? Then we could have the whole school coming over to see Cadillac," I grumbled.

Sprinting ahead when the policeman beckoned us to cross, I thought I could shake them. But everyone ran along behind me. I felt like the Pied Piper. The nearer I got to home, the more worried I became. Had Mom spent the day getting a hen and a cow to keep Cadillac company? How long was this pig phase going to last anyway? All last winter she'd kept us tramping over Plum Island looking for snowy owls.

Everything looked very peaceful when we reached 37 Pinecrest Drive. I led the troops in the front door. We found Mom in the kitchen lifting chocolate chip cookies from a cookie sheet and putting them on racks to cool. Each cookie was perfectly browned and bulging with lumps of chocolate. The kitchen smelled good again.

Twinky Rogers took his cap pistol out of its holster on his belt and shot at the moose head on the wall in the family room. "Got ya," he said, replacing the pistol in the holster.

Christine didn't waste time on preliminaries. "Where's the pig?"

"Out in the yard with Olivia."

I could see from the window that Olivia was sitting on the ground pretending to read to Cadillac from her Mother Goose book. The pig's head rested in her lap.

Everyone but me scooped up cookies and spilled out into the yard. I scooped up cookies and retreated to my room to read *The Story of Baseball,* hoping to spend the entire afternoon on it.

But I didn't have that kind of luck. Mom poked her head in the door after I'd read just a few pages. "Keep your eye on the kids, will you? I have to get groceries. Clarence Matthew is taking a nap. I should be home by the time he wakes up."

I didn't have a chance to open my mouth before she was gone. Good old Terry comes to the rescue again. I slammed my book shut and raided the kitchen for more cookies. If I was going to baby-sit a mob of kids, I was going to do it on a full stomach.

The cellar door opened. Joel and Twinky appeared, dragging a plastic trash can after them.

"What are you doing?"

"Nothing."

"If you dump trash all over the yard, you're going to pick it up."

Joel took the cover off the can. "It's empty."

"Be good, will ya? I've got better things to do than trail after you all afternoon."

Joel and Twinky hauled the can outside. I opened the kitchen window and brought my book to the table. That way I could read and still hear anyone who cried. Let's see, where was I?

Joel ran down cellar again and came up in a few minutes with a long rope. He took it out to the yard. I heard a lot of yelling and screaming, but it sounded harmless.

When I heard someone call, "How many minutes to lift-off?" I wondered what was going on. Maybe I'd better check.

Coming into the backyard, I saw that a tall aluminum ladder was set up under the maple tree. The trash can was perched on top of the ladder. The long rope was tied to one of the handles of the can and draped over a high branch of the tree. Joel and Twinky were standing on the ground hanging on to the end of the rope.

The space center technicians, bunched at the foot of the ladder, chanted, "10, 9, 8, 7, 6, 5, 4, 3, 2, 1, 0. Ignition. BLAST OFF!"

Joel and Twinky pulled the rope and lifted the plastic can off the ladder. "To Mars!"

"Hurray!" yelled ground control.

Slowly the can rose into the air. Why wasn't it moving faster? Had Joel filled it with rocks? Up toward the top of the tree it climbed as the boys strained to raise it higher and higher and—The rope slipped! The can fell, hit a low branch, and tipped. Off flew the lid and out of the can sailed Cadillac.

5. Kaiser and the Garbage

I ran forward. "Joel, are you trying to kill that pig?"

Cadillac shot over the fence and splashed down in a basket of clean sheets that Mrs. Wilson, next door on the right, was taking off her clothesline.

Mrs. Wilson let out a screech. With the junior spacemen hot on my heels, I rushed into her yard to retrieve Cadillac.

Cadillac didn't wait to be rescued. He was out of the basket, out of the yard, and down the street, a squealing streak of fright.

"Faster than a speeding bullet, it's Super Pig!" Twinky yelled.

"For Lord's sakes, can't you kids keep your crazy animals in your own yard?"

"Cadillac's only a sweet little pig who wouldn't hurt a flea," Olivia told her.

Carrying her laundry basket, Mrs. Wilson stormed into her house and slammed the door.

The gang lit out after the pig.

"Hold it! Hold it, everybody!" I gathered the army for a strategy session. "We're never going to catch that pig if we chase him."

"Call the police."

"Call the firemen."

"Cadillac isn't a cat up in a tree, you jokers," I told them. I wasn't sure what to do, but I had to come up with something quick. What would Mom do? Soft words and food, that was her way. It was worth a try.

"Olivia, get Cadillac's pan from the backyard. The rest of you, go home and bring back whatever garbage you can find. Don't yell. Don't run. We've got to soothe that pig. I'm going to walk around quietly and try to find out where he's hiding."

Everyone scattered. Joel started to follow Twinky down the street.

"Joel, wait a minute. Go back to the house and stay there."

"Why?"

"I forgot that Clarence Matthew is alone."

"You go back if you're worried about him."

"I've got to find the pig."

"I'll find Cadillac. You check on the baby."

"Look, Joel, you're the one who got us into this

33

mess. If I leave you in charge, you'll louse everything up."

"I'm not going back."

"Do you want your baby brother to burn up?"

"Did you leave him in the oven?"

"Of course I didn't leave him in the oven." I wanted to smack Joel, but I knew that wouldn't help, so I tried another tack. "Joel, you're the only one I can trust with the job."

"I don't want to be trusted. I want to run after Cadillac. Get Olivia to stay with the baby."

"You are older and smarter than Olivia. She is just a baby herself. *You* can defy death by pulling your baby brother out of the flames."

"Why did you set him on fire?"

I could feel my voice getting out of control. "I didn't set him on fire, dummy. I'm just talking about what could happen."

"Then how am I supposed to pull him out of the flames?"

"Just go and make sure Clarence Matthew is all right. Make sure he doesn't fall out of his crib or anything. You can come back the instant Mom comes home."

"I don't want to go."

"Please, Joel."

"But—"

"GO!"

Joel trudged back to our yard, and I stood on the sidewalk trying to figure out where to go first. Mrs.

Wilson's sleek white cat, Lily, sat on her front steps in the sun, eyeing me, slowly swishing her tail.

Pinecrest Drive is a dead-end street that runs off Washington Avenue. I hoped the pig was still on Pinecrest. Washington has a lot of traffic because it leads straight into the center of town. I hated the thought of nosing around every yard on our street. But I had to do something. I couldn't abandon Cadillac.

Looking at every shrub and bush, trying to decide where I would hide if I were a little pig, I walked slowly down Pinecrest Drive.

Halfway down the street was Mrs. Carver's house, set back farther from the road than the other houses, with laurel and rhododendron bushes covering up most of the front of the house. Those bushes would be a good hiding place. Mrs. Carver was old and could only walk with someone helping her. She wouldn't notice if I checked around her shrubs.

I was on my hands and knees peering under the laurel when I heard a window fly up and someone yell, "Get out of there!" I had forgotten about Mrs. Snyder, Mrs. Carver's companion.

I felt as if I had been caught trying to steal her silver. "I'm looking for my pig, Mrs. Snyder." It sounded ridiculous.

"Well, it's not under those bushes."

Olivia ran up, holding the yellow plastic dish proudly in front of her. It was mounded with smelly garbage. Apple peelings dripped over the sides.

"What are you planning to do with that garbage?" Mrs. Snyder's voice was as friendly as a guard dog's growl.

"Sorry to bother you," I said, pushing Olivia toward the street.

"If you see a little white pig, you tell us, okay?" Olivia said pleasantly.

"You kids play in your own yard." Slam. The window was closed and locked.

Twinky, Jimmy, and the Foster twins were waiting on the sidewalk. Christine and Chucky had disappeared.

"Let's look on the other side of the street," Jimmy suggested.

Why hadn't I thought of that? The Rogerses, the Fosters, and the Pomeroys lived on that side and we could snoop around those yards all we wanted. "Now remember, no running, no yelling. We want Cadillac to stay where he is. When we find him, we'll lure him home with the garbage."

I was amazed—the kids actually did what I told them. We looked under every tree, behind every bush, beside the porches, but Cadillac seemed to have vanished. Discouraged, we flopped down on the Pomeroys' back steps to rest.

"Somebody's going to have a free pork roast tonight," I said.

"You want to play baseball, Terry?" Jimmy asked.

I always want to play baseball. "Get your bat and glove and ball," I said, "and I'll show you some pitching techniques I've been working on."

Jimmy ran into the garage and popped out again, grinning, motioning us to come. There was Cadillac, crouched in the corner behind three big bags of fertilizer.

"Out, all of you," I said as quietly as I could. "Go over to my house and wait there."

I put the pan of garbage in the door of the garage, then positioned myself out of the way, but nearby. I started talking to Cadillac in the tone of voice Mom uses when we're hurt or upset. "There, there, that's a good pig. Come get some nice, juicy, sloppy garbage. Apple peelings, banana skins. Yum, yum."

Cadillac didn't take long to move toward the dish. Just before he reached it, I picked it up slowly and carried it down the driveway a little beyond his reach. He trotted after me and I led him onto the sidewalk.

We were crossing in front of Miss Dowd's house, with only a few more feet to go before we reached our yard, when Kaiser charged toward us, woof-woofing as if he intended to rip us apart.

Cadillac disappeared again before I had a chance to grab him. My blood pressure shot up to a thousand. Kaiser is the neighborhood bully. He chases us every time we go off on our bikes, running beside us, barking up a storm. When we're walking he's liable to stand in the middle of the sidewalk, growling, not letting us get past him.

Joel had gotten a new ski jacket last winter and the first time he put it on, Kaiser grabbed the back of it in his teeth and ripped it. Of course Kaiser is supposed to be tied up, but Miss Dowd lets him run loose most of the time.

So when that savage beast frightened Cadillac, all of us got so mad we forgot about the pig for a minute and went after Kaiser, yelling at the top of our lungs. Jimmy had his baseball bat in his hands and he swung it in the air near the dog. I still had the pan of garbage. Without thinking, I emptied it over Kaiser's head.

6. "You've Got Some Nerve . . ."

Growling, Kaiser retreated. All of us stood on the sidewalk and laughed—we were so glad to see him get what was coming to him for once. But we didn't laugh long.

Miss Dowd flew out of her house like a hurricane. "Get away. Get away before I call the police."

We backed into the street.

"Hoodlums. That what you are. Hoodlums. Nothing to do but throw garbage around."

Miss Dowd's lawn was a mess. Grapefruit rinds, banana skins, apple peelings, scraps of wilted lettuce, and globs of heaven-knows-what were strewn all over one section of it. I wished I hadn't gotten so mad.

"You ought to be locked up, all of you. Destroying property like that."

I took a step forward. "I'm sorry, Miss Dowd. It's my fault. I'll clean it up."

The next ten minutes seemed like ten years. The other kids helped and I didn't even have to ask them. We threw the globby, smelly yuck back into the pan. Miss Dowd raved on all the time we were clearing up, like a one-woman thunderstorm.

We cleaned up everything we could and then I hitched up a hose and washed away the rest. We all went home to our separate houses. I was so miserable about the garbage incident that I had forgotten about the pig.

Olivia hadn't forgotten. She was in tears. "Please, Terry, please help me find him."

"I'm not moving out of this house until tomorrow. That pig has made enough trouble for me for one day."

"We can't just leave him to die!"

"I'm not moving and that's that."

Mom came home while we were still arguing. She had stopped off at Whittier Place, where the backyards on the odd-numbered side back up to the even-numbered yards on Pinecrest Drive. Mom gets groceries for Mrs. Hansen, who can't drive, and when she drove into Mrs. Hansen's driveway she spotted Cadillac and cornered him, bright red and shaking from fright, in the garage.

Olivia was so glad to see Cadillac again that she cradled him in her arms and lugged him into the family room.

"You can comfort him inside for a few minutes,

dear. Then he'll have to go outside again," Mom told her.

We told Mom that Cadillac had run out through the gate when it was open. We thought we could keep her from finding out the whole story. That was ridiculous —before she had finished putting away the groceries, Miss Dowd was on our doorstep.

"Well!"

"Amelia, how nice to see you. Come have a cup of coffee. I've just perked a fresh pot."

"I don't pay taxes to have garbage dumped all over my lawn."

A rich coffee aroma floated out from the kitchen. "Doesn't that smell wonderful, Amelia? Come in and have a cup," Mom said, leading the way into the kitchen.

I pretended to be watching TV in the family room with Joel and Olivia, but I was eyeing Miss Dowd, hoping she wouldn't spot Cadillac. He was back to his normal color now and he lay on his side on the sofa, his head tight against Olivia while she scratched his stomach.

Setting a steaming cup of coffee in front of Miss Dowd, Mom said, "Cream and sugar?"

"Black. Children aren't brought up the way they should be these days. Let me tell you, I'd have been spanked if I had poured garbage on someone's property."

My mother took a long, slow sip of her coffee. "Maybe you had better start from the beginning."

"You have no idea how frightening it was to see all those young rowdies beating up my poor Kaiser. It's a good thing I happened to look out the window just then. There's no telling what they would have done if I hadn't stopped them."

"Was Kaiser running after the children?"

"That's just the trouble with you parents. Always think someone else is to blame."

I couldn't sit still any longer. I went into the kitchen and in as few words as possible explained how we had tried to find Cadillac and bring him home. Before I could get to the part about Kaiser, Miss Dowd interrupted.

"What's the matter with your children, Ethel? Why are they out chasing Cadillacs? How do you expect them to grow into decent citizens if they spend their time trying to steal cars?"

Mom laughed. "Amelia, you don't understand. The Cadillac Terry is talking about is not a car. It's a baby pig."

I don't know what possessed Olivia, but she carried the pig, wearing one of Clarence Matthew's diapers, out to the kitchen. "See, Miss Dowd, isn't he cute? And your awful Kaiser scared him."

Miss Dowd fingered the pin that she always wore on a frayed brown ribbon around her neck. Mom told me the pin was a cameo. It looked like a tiny picture—the white face of a lady on a black stone in a gold frame.

Olivia kept talking. "He's severely intelligent. He

42

figured out how to open up the cupboard doors in our kitchen."

Miss Dowd clutched her cameo. "Are you keeping pigs in your house, Ethel?"

"One. He lives in the backyard. In the fenced-in area. We'll be sure the gate is closed from now on so he can't get out again."

Miss Dowd rose from the table. "Keeping pigs in your house! I never heard of such a thing. This neighborhood is going down, down, down. All I can say is, you've got some nerve, Ethel Blodgett, running for the School Board. I'll never vote for you, and I intend to see that no one else votes for you either."

7. Mom Takes a Stand

I could hardly swallow my supper that night. Mom looked as if nothing had happened. I couldn't understand her.

"Everything will be all right if you get rid of that pig," I told her.

"I have no intention of getting rid of Cadillac, at least not right away."

"You know Miss Dowd got on the phone the minute she left here, talking to everyone in town about us."

"Terry, how did Cadillac get out of the yard?"

"Joel and Twinky—"

Joel rushed to defend himself. "It was Jimmy's idea."

"Yeah, I'll bet. You're the one who's so crazy about space."

Mom interrupted. "Boys!" Before long she had the

44

whole story. No one noticed that Olivia hadn't put Cadillac outdoors at suppertime. I was too mad to notice anything. I hate Mom's projects, and I hate the way I always end up getting involved in them.

I don't give a raw turnip about ancient Egypt, but last fall she made me help her build a huge balsa wood pyramid in the basement, and she dragged Joel and me all over the Boston Museum of Fine Arts, lecturing us about mummies. If she'd only talk about baseball once in a while, I'd be interested in listening.

Why can't she listen to *me* when I talk about the batting averages of players in the major leagues? But no. Every time I try to talk baseball with her she gets this glazed look in her eyes and says, "Mmmmmmmmm, mnnnnnnn," so I know she's thinking about something completely different.

"Children, clean up the kitchen, please, while I put Clarence Matthew to bed."

My stomach was so knotted it began to ache. I wished I could lie down, but I took a load of dishes off the table. Olivia wasn't anywhere around and Joel had sneaked off to watch TV in the family room.

"Joel, you little jerk, why don't you help out?"

Mom came back in the kitchen to get the baby's pacifier. "That's no way to talk to your brother."

"I'm twisted into a pretzel with stomach cramps and you expect me to talk to him like he's superintendent of schools? Joel dear, if it isn't too much trouble, would you please honor me with your presence in the kitchen *before I beat you into mashed potatoes?*"

45

"Mama, come quick," Olivia called. "Cadillac's chewing your garden up."

We found the pig happily munching the baby plants under the bay window in the living room. He had nosed around the pots, upsetting them. Dirt was spilled all over the floor and was crushed into the rug by his feet as he tasted a few tomato plants, a few beans, zucchini here, broccoli there.

I helped with the kitchen, but I didn't lift a finger to clean up the living room. I'd had it with that pig.

When I climbed into bed that night and turned out the light, I heard voices outside on the sidewalk. My room faces the street, so I always hear people coming and going.

"You're right, Jan."

Was that Mr. Pomeroy's voice? I crept over to the window in the dark and peered out. In the yellow circle of the streetlight I saw the Pomeroys talking to the Wilsons. Mrs. Snyder was walking down the street with the Fosters. The whole neighborhood was out.

Everyone seemed to be coming from Miss Dowd's house. She wasn't one to throw parties. Why had she brought everyone together?

I didn't have to wait long to find out. Mrs. Pomeroy was on the phone to Mom at eight the next morning.

"No, Jan, I'm not upset. Should I be?"

I couldn't hear Mrs. Pomeroy's words, but I could hear her tone of voice—it almost cracked my cereal bowl. Mom held the receiver several inches away from her ear.

46

"Don't make any plans for the next two weeks, Terry," she said when she hung up. "I'm going to need all the help I can get for my campaign."

That made me so mad I almost choked on my corn-flakes. *I* wasn't interested in running for the School Board. I wasn't particularly interested in having Mom run. If she won, I'd see her less and I'd have to do more work around the house. Why should I give up my free time for the next two weeks to do something I didn't believe in?

By the time I reached school I felt like a firecracker waiting for a match. A couple of jokers greeted me with, "Hey, Piggy!" and "Oink, oink!" I ignored them. But when Toby Phitz yelled, "Got your garbage for lunch, Terry?" I grabbed him by the collar and slammed him down on the ground.

Unfortunately, Mr. Adams was checking on the buses and he saw what happened. "Terry, that's not the way we act at Longfellow School. I'm surprised at you."

I was surprised at myself. I don't usually react that violently.

Toby got up, rubbing his head. "He pushed me down for no reason."

I thought I had plenty of reason but I didn't say that.

"You owe Toby an apology, Terry," Mr. Adams said.

After mumbling something insincere about being sorry, I stalked into the building, feeling terrible. People were beginning to notice me, but not in the way I wanted.

As soon as school began, Mrs. Lambartini made me feel worse. "We're all looking forward to your report on pigs this Friday," she said, smiling sweetly. The rest of the morning I daydreamed about shipping Mrs. Lambartini off to a candy factory and dropping her into a vat of peppermint. When she was melted down and wrapped in cellophane, I would eat her up—slowly. She'd probably taste like steel, though, not sugar.

In the lunchroom Christine Pomeroy sidled up to me and said, "My father says you're lowering the value of every home on our street by keeping a dirty pig around."

That made me sizzle again. Cadillac was no friend of mine and I wanted to get rid of him as much as anyone else, but it seemed to me that Kaiser lowered the value of houses on Pinecrest Drive more than our little pig.

I spent part of the afternoon in the school library preparing for my report. The thing that surprised me most was how little information I could find about pigs. There were books on hamsters and parakeets and kangaroos, but nothing on pigs. Only the encyclopedias had any information on them. Did everyone think they were too dirty to think about? The encyclopedia said they were the most intelligent of domestic animals and were as clean as their owners allowed them to be.

After supper that night, Mr. Pomeroy showed up at our house. "Hear you've got an addition to your family, Ethel," he began, smiling his smooth salesman's smile.

"You might say that, Stan. Cup of coffee? I've got

some elegant apple pie I made this afternoon. Want a piece?"

Mr. Pomeroy put his hand over his stomach. "Just finished eating, thanks." He sat down at the kitchen table, pulling up the knees of his carefully pressed slacks. His shoes were as glossy as black marble. I put my dishes on the counter and followed Joel into the family room to watch TV.

"I guess you know," Mr. Pomeroy said, "you need a permit to have a farm animal on your premises."

I turned down the volume on the TV so I could hear the conversation in the kitchen clearly. Maybe Mr. Pomeroy could bring this pig business to a halt.

"Our pig is not a permanent fixture, Stan," Mom told him.

"How long do you plan to keep him?"

I strained to hear the answer to that. "Just long enough to let the children get acquainted with him."

"He created quite an uproar on the street yesterday."

"Most of that uproar was due to the dog who lives permanently on this street and has a history of bullying your children and mine."

"That may be so, but—"

"There are regulations about dogs, too, Stan. Regulations that have never been properly observed."

"A single woman like Amelia needs a dog for protection."

Mom had heard that argument before and she wasn't swayed by it. "Kaiser is protection against a good night's sleep. You know you've been kept awake many a night by his barking."

"Amelia isn't running for the School Board. You are. You've got to get rid of that pig, Ethel. If you pack it off tomorrow, this will all blow over before the election."

I had never thought of Mr. Pomeroy as a special friend, but I did now. If only Mom would listen to him, maybe everyone in school would start thinking of me as the guy who plays an excellent game of baseball instead of the kid with the pig.

"Stan, I will not cave in under this kind of pressure."

I groaned—I knew it was all over. Mr. Pomeroy didn't, though. He kept arguing, and Mom wouldn't give an inch.

"I suppose you're going to claim that your civil rights are being violated if you can't have a pig stinking up the whole neighborhood. Let me tell you one thing. Jan and I are leaving your campaign as of this minute. We're not giving our time to work for someone who refuses to consider the rights of other people."

8. Slamming in a Home Run

My mother fools people. She's overweight and she smiles a lot. She's very friendly and she's always doing something to help someone. So everyone thinks she's a jolly Mrs. Santa Claus who's easy to manage.

But they are wrong. If Mom thinks she's fighting for a Great Principle, she's as determined as a bulldozer and nothing can stop her.

For a long time that night, I lay in bed not able to sleep. Ever since the pig had come to 37 Pinecrest Drive, things had happened so fast I felt I was on a roller coaster. I wanted to yell, "Stop! Let me off!"

Mrs. Pomeroy had been Mom's campaign manager and Mr. Pomeroy had been her treasurer. If neither of them would work for her, that meant she would have a hard time doing all the extra work herself. I could see the handwriting on the wall. She would ask me to do all the things she didn't have time to do, and I'd have no time for myself at all. No time to practice pitching and batting and sliding into base before the Little League tryouts a week from Saturday.

What made my teeth really grind was knowing how Mom would give me a big pep talk about "learning the political system firsthand" and "broadening my interests." Somehow I had to get control of things.

The next morning I was up by six thirty. I planned on getting my own breakfast and leaving for school early. When I came down to the kitchen I found Mom already dressed, humming, full of energy, rustling up a big breakfast of blueberry muffins, scrambled eggs, and bacon. Clarence Matthew was sitting in his high chair, banging on the tray with a spoon and yelling, "Da, da, da!"

"Did you know, Terry, pigs are so intelligent that during the war they were trained to sniff out land mines? Now they're used in France to find truffles. They can sniff out a truffle ten inches under the ground from twenty feet away. A pig's nose is much more sensitive than a dog's." Mom set down a half grapefruit in front of me so hard that it bounced up from the plate.

I wanted to ask what a truffle was, but I decided to look it up in the dictionary later. I *refused* to act interested in anything that had to do with *her* pig.

I ran off to school, not waiting for Joel, barely taking time to say good-by to Mom. I mumbled something about having work to do before school and was out the door before she could question me.

Outside the drugstore at the corner of East and Washington was a phone booth. I slipped into it and dialed Gramp's number. I had thought of calling long distance to Dad. I wasn't sure, though, what hotel he was staying in. Besides, I thought there was a wild chance Mom would listen to her own father when she wouldn't listen to anyone else.

Gramp has a hearing problem, but I finally made him understand why I was calling. "You've got to talk to Mom," I shouted into the phone. "She's got to get rid of that pig. She'll lose the election if she doesn't."

Gramp promised to call Mom, but I hung up feeling I hadn't convinced him how serious things were.

Christine Pomeroy passed me when I came out of the phone booth. "Hi," I said casually. "How'd you do with the math problems we had for homework last night?"

She didn't answer me, just tossed her hair back and walked a little faster.

While I was wondering what was eating her, Toby Phitz spotted me. "Well, if it isn't Piggy. What's the price of bacon, Pig?"

I wanted to belt him, but I kept my cool. I had to separate myself from that pig and let people know it was my mother's project not mine.

Right after the Pledge of Allegiance I had my chance. Mrs. Lambartini said, "We're looking forward to your report on pigs tomorrow, Terry. Remember, don't just recite a lot of facts. Try to give your presentation a little flair."

I imagined myself giving a talk entitled "The Pig, Man's Best Friend." I'd show how every part of a pig has some use. I'd have a brush made from pig bristles, and pickled pig's feet for the class to sample. Best of all, I'd get a pig's intestine, hold it up, and explain how it was used to hold sausage meat. That would really get Christine. She would probably throw up right on the spot and never be able to eat sausage again.

"We don't have the opportunity to see a live farm animal every day," Mrs. Lambartini continued, her face spreading into a sticky-jam smile.

That smile gave me the push I needed. "I'm not going to give the report, Mrs. Lambartini."

"What did you say?"

I kept my voice respectful. "I'm not going to give the pig report."

My classmates were hushed, like spectators at a boxing match waiting to see if a fighter will stay down after a knockout.

"Of course you'll give your report."

"Is this a requirement? Does everyone have to report on some animal?"

"Well, no. It's for extra credit. It'll help bring up your science grade."

"I've decided not to do it."

"Terry, this isn't like you."

You're right, I thought. This is a new Terry Blodgett.

Someone who thinks for himself for a change instead of being led around like a puppy. I felt suddenly bigger.

"I'll have to give your mother a call."

"That's fine." No one could say I was being fresh.

Mrs. Lambartini went to her desk, wrote down something, then switched the attention of the class to the use of adverbs.

I realized then that I'd have to face my mother the same way I'd faced Mrs. Lambartini. Mom was big on "having the courage of your convictions." She should be proud of me. I'd be very calm. Calm but firm.

When I got home from school that afternoon, Mom greeted me with, "What's this about your refusing to give your science report?"

I didn't have a chance to answer. The doorbell interrupted us. A short, round, gray-haired man had come to call. Mr. Muggridge, the Town Sanitarian, from the Board of Health.

If Mom was upset, she didn't show it. She smiled welcomingly and led him into the kitchen where she offered him a raspberry tart.

No one could refuse them. They were fresh from the oven and the smell of them made your mouth water.

Mr. Muggridge reached out a plump hand eagerly. "I haven't had a raspberry tart in years. Mmmm-mmmmmmm. Delicious. My!"

"Have another."

"Don't mind if I do. Such flaky crust. Thank you."

He finally got around to discussing Cadillac. "I brought along a copy of our regulations concerning horses, cows, goats, swine, sheep, and poultry. Chapter 9. You see it says here in Section 1 that you need a permit."

"I'm afraid I didn't realize that, Mr. Muggridge. You see, we aren't planning to raise him. You might say he's a temporary guest."

"That puts a different complexion on the matter. But we've had complaints from your neighbors, you know."

"Let me show you the provisions we've made for the pig. You can tell me if they're adequate."

"You'll have to keep the pen free from decaying food, filth, dirt, and stagnant water."

I followed them outside. There sat Gramp on one of the picnic benches, with Olivia in his lap. A spotless Cadillac was busy retrieving a ball that Joel tossed a few feet away. A new wire fence had been put up around Cadillac's house, giving him a separate yard to run in.

"My father helped me put up that fence just today," Mom said.

Mr. Muggridge stood by the fence gabbing with Mom, watching Cadillac. I watched Cadillac, too. We all did. He's a smart pig. Every time he brought the ball back to Joel, Joel gave him a corn muffin. But one time he didn't. Joel held his hands out flat to show he had nothing in them. Cadillac sniffed at them, sniffed all around where Joel was standing, then trotted over to the fence to sniff at the paper bag that had held the muffins.

That gave Joel an idea. He got a fistful of cookies

from the house and handed them to me, except for one, which he fed Cadillac. Then he carried Cadillac into his house and told me to hide the cookies in the yard.

When Joel brought the pig out of the house again, he located every one of those cookies in no time.

"That's a splendid little pig," Mr. Muggridge said as he left, giving Mom an application to fill out for a permit. "I'll have a talk with your neighbors."

I was disgusted. Why couldn't Mr. Muggridge have told Mom to get rid of the pig immediately? If we kept him much longer, the kids in school were likely to think up names for me like Sausage Brain, and Pickled Pork Face.

When Mom drove Gramp back to his apartment she took Olivia and Clarence Matthew with her. I stayed outside in the yard with Joel trying to figure out how to get rid of Cadillac.

Maybe I could sneak out in the middle of the night and butcher him. That was so funny I laughed out loud. We'd had a mouse in our cellar once and I couldn't bear to set the trap for it or look at it when it was caught. So it wasn't likely that I'd be able to do away with anything like a pig.

Maybe I could convince Mr. Pomeroy to help me kidnap Cadillac. Sometime when Mom wasn't around we'd grab him, shove him into Mr. Pomeroy's car, and drive him back to the farm.

I watched Cadillac scratching his back against a fencepost. When he had taken care of his itch, he turned and looked at me, not the way a dog looks, begging for affection or a handout, or as if he intends to tear you to bits. No, Cadillac looked at me in a steady, considering sort of way, as if he and I were equals.

Crazy pig. I tossed a clothespin at him and ran into the house to get my bat, ball, and glove. A little batting practice might help me forget my problems.

I didn't have any trouble talking Joel into playing with me—he likes baseball almost as much as I do. Joel wound up and threw a fast ball, a little low. I swung and missed. Strike one. Another fast ball. Another strike. For a minute we weren't on Pinecrest Drive. We were in Fenway Park playing the last game of the World Series.

It was the bottom of the ninth. The score was tied, the bases loaded. I stood poised at the plate, ready for anything. The pitch came, high and outside. I swung and hit, slamming the ball right out of the park. The fans were on their feet cheering as I ran to first, to second, to third. Home. The crowd went wild.

The sound of shattering glass brought me back to reality. My hit had smashed one of Miss Dowd's side windows. I prayed it hadn't hit her.

9. Mom Interferes

Miss Dowd didn't ring the doorbell when she came —she hammered with the door knocker. Kaiser was with her.

Mom wouldn't let the dog in. "He frightens the little children terribly."

"You don't mind living with filthy swine, but you object to a good clean dog. Don't you think I'm frightened to have baseballs come flying through my windows?" Her hand closed over the cameo on the worn brown ribbon around her neck. We certainly weren't going to steal it, but she clutched it as if she thought we might.

Mom tried to pacify her, saying she would pay for new glass and arrange for someone to install it. She had forbidden us to play baseball in the yard any more.

Miss Dowd still went away mad. I was thankful my ball hadn't knocked her unconscious.

Would she call the police when she got home and ask them to haul us off to jail for disturbing the peace or for unlawful possession of a pig?

I could picture the whole scene. Lights flashing, sirens wailing, a police car would roar up Pinecrest Drive and a couple of burly officers would shove us into their car. Then they'd pack us all into a cell like a closet with no windows, and there we'd sit, living on bread and water, until Dad could get us released on bail. The newspapers would run a picture of Mom with the caption "Pig Woman Sent to Pen."

The police didn't come. We had a quiet supper during which I became more and more nervous waiting for Mom to bring up the pig report for school.

Dad telephoned. Mom didn't let us talk to him very long. I think she was afraid we'd tell him what had been happening. She sounded calm and gay as she told him everything was going just fine. How could she lie like that?

Mom seemed to have forgotten about my report. She rushed out after supper to attend a coffee some lady at the other end of Brookside was giving for her. I was left to baby-sit.

By breakfast time the next morning I was sure I'd heard the last about my pig report when Mom stopped in the middle of frying eggs to say, "Your teacher was at the coffee last night, Terry. We had a long talk after the others left and decided that I would give your science report."

I dropped the piece of toast in my hand. *"You're going to come into my classroom to give my report?"*

"Not in your classroom. Mrs. Lambartini is going to speak to Mr. Adams to see if I can talk to two or three classes in the cafetorium."

Did I dare hope that Mr. Adams would refuse to give permission to bring the pig in? Not a chance. Everyone at school loves Mom. The teachers are always telling me how fortunate I am to have a mother who provides so many "enriching experiences" outside school.

"You always do things for Terry's class. Why can't you talk to my class?" Joel whined.

Mom reached over and hugged him. "I'm going to try to give a talk to the second-graders, too, and maybe other classes."

One last faint hope of getting Mom to stay home flickered across my mind. "Clarence Matthew has to have a nap in the afternoon. How are you going to get a baby-sitter during the day? Gramp volunteers to work in the library every Friday."

"Mrs. Hansen may be willing to stay with the little ones."

My heart sank. Mrs. Hansen loved Olivia and Clarence Matthew and she felt indebted to Mom for taking her shopping every week.

Couldn't Mom see how miserable she was making me? Couldn't she see that I'd be humiliated in front of the whole school if she brought Cadillac in? The kids would never stop calling me Piggy and oinking every time I got near them.

"I'll never be elected baseball captain now!"

"If learning about pigs is going to prevent your friends from electing you baseball captain, then being baseball captain isn't important."

I jumped up from the table. "Maybe it's not important to you, but it's important to me."

"You have to pay a price for your convictions, Terry."

"They're not *my* convictions. Why do I have to suffer for *your* convictions?"

"Pigs are very fascinating," Olivia said, parroting Mother.

"Why don't you just mind your own business!"

"She's right, Terry," Mother said.

"I don't care. I don't want you bringing that foolish pig into school. My friends know all they need to know about hogs."

"That's where you're wrong. People *think* they know about pigs, but they don't. They think pigs are stupid and dirty. But they're not. That's why I need to come in and talk to the children."

Mom was so calm and logical. Why didn't she scream like other mothers? Then I could tune her out like a radio.

"Miss Dowd has probably been telling everyone why you shouldn't be elected to the School Board. Probably the Pomeroys have been talking, too. If you go to school with Cadillac, all the kids will go home and tell their parents. Then the whole town will know we have a pig at our house."

"And they'll know what's true and what isn't true about pigs."

I couldn't stand any more talking. I picked up my jacket and books and bolted for the door.

"You forgot your lunch money," Mom called after me.

I didn't go back after it. I didn't care whether I ate lunch or not. My day was already ruined.

Jeff Higgins came up to me while I was throwing a few balls against the side of the school building as I waited for the first bell. "How're things goin' down on the farm, Piggy? Need any help with the milkin'?"

"Shut up!"

"You gonna bring your little pig in to show us?"

I swung at him, but he ducked and laughed. Where was that cool confidence I'd had yesterday? I wished I knew how to get it back.

10. Another Chase

Since I couldn't keep Mom from coming to school, I tried to think of a way of not being there when she arrived. Maybe I could faint.

I'd groan, shut my eyes, and keel over. Everyone would rush over to me yelling, "Terry, what's wrong?" I wouldn't answer. I'd just lie there, eyes closed, mouth lax, still as a corpse. Someone would yell, "Quick, call the ambulance! Get him to the hospital before it's too late . . ."

My daydream evaporated. If I tried to faint, it would be just my luck to hit something when I fell, so that I'd break my wrist or my arm and be out of baseball for the season.

Mrs. Lambartini lent me money for lunch, so I was able to eat after all. By one o'clock Mom hadn't shown up. Had she decided not to come after all?

That hope died fast. Christine Pomeroy went to the front of the room near the windows to sharpen her pencil. On her way back to her seat she passed me and hissed, "Your mother is here. She's carrying a suitcase."

I shrugged and tried to keep my face a blank. Inside, though, I felt like yelling swear words.

In a few minutes we filed down to the cafetorium. That's the combination cafeteria and auditorium. I considered darting out of the line and hiding somewhere until my class went back to our room. But I knew I'd be caught. So I plodded along with everyone else. I felt like a prisoner of war being led to the firing squad. In a few minutes my dream of being captain of a baseball team would be dead. Who could like or respect a kid whose mother brought a pig to school?

Mom had put on makeup and a bright-red blouse and scarf. She smiled and tried to catch my eye, but I pretended I didn't know her. She told the classes to sit on the floor in a half circle facing her and the "suitcase," which was an animal carrying case that she must have rented from the pet store. I chose a spot on the side, where I hoped I was inconspicuous.

You could tell that Mom had been a teacher, because she wasn't one bit nervous and she knew just how to catch everyone's attention. She told us things about pigs that made even me sit up and listen.

Pigs, she said, can be taught anything that a dog can learn and will learn it faster. A sow, two hundred years ago in England, figured out how to find game birds for hunters by watching the bird dogs. After a while she was better at hunting than the dogs.

Lots of farmers keep hogs near ponds where their cows drink. Why? To gobble up the snakes that might bite the cattle. Even when the pigs gulp down poisonous snakes they don't get sick or die. Their fat protects them from the poison.

Mom opened up the carrying case. Cadillac poked his head out and looked at us with his sharp little eyes. Mom scratched behind his ears while she talked to him in a gentle, soothing voice.

When she lifted him out and set him on the floor, he peered at all of us, then hid behind Mom, who was kneeling on the floor beside him. In a minute, though, he peeked around at us, ducked back, peeked out again.

Olivia must have spent all morning scrubbing him. You never saw such a sparkling pink-and-white pig. He looked as if he had stepped out of a picture book, except that he wasn't wearing clothes.

Before long, Cadillac was satisfied that we weren't going to hurt him and he showed how he could fetch. Mom rolled a small rubber ball across the floor. He trotted after it, picked it up in his mouth, and dropped it in front of Mom, who rewarded him with a stale doughnut.

Next, Mom put him back in the carrying case and hid a doughnut behind the lost-and-found box. Then she took Cadillac out and said, "You're a smart pig, go find the doughnut."

66

He looked up at her as if he understood, sniffed around, and in no time discovered the hidden doughnut.

"Let's try one more trick," Mom said, as she untied the silk scarf from her neck and put it under Cadillac's nose. She closed him in the case again and hid the scarf under the upright piano.

"Go find my scarf," she said as she unfastened the case.

I think Cadillac thought she had hidden more food. He nosed around and when he came near to where the scarf was hidden, Mom pulled it out, patted and scratched him, and fed him another doughnut. Cadillac looked very pleased with himself.

He began to show off then, trotting fast across the smooth waxed floor, braking to a stop, then sliding on his hoofs exactly as if he were on ice.

The audience clapped and cheered. "Hey, how about that." "Isn't he cute?" "I wish I had a pig." "That's some animal."

I sighed with relief. Maybe my classmates would think of me now as the guy with the interesting pet instead of the kooky kid with the pig.

A minute later everything was changed. The custodian propped open the door into the kitchen, grabbed a full trash barrel, heaved it onto his shoulder, and headed through the kitchen to the trash bins outside.

At that instant the fire alarm sounded. Cadillac panicked and ran. Mom grabbed for him, but she wasn't quick enough. He made a beeline for the open kitchen door, with me after him.

"Watch out for the pig!" I yelled, trying to make myself heard above the ear-splitting alarm. Everyone, Mom included, hurried toward the regular fire exits. Except me. Fire or no fire, I had to catch Cadillac.

As I came charging into the kitchen, the custodian stopped for a second and turned to see what was happening. I smacked right into him. Crumpled napkins, disposable plates, and empty milk cartons from the barrel on his shoulder rained over me.

I didn't stop. I just plowed on after Cadillac, who tripped up a lunch worker carrying a gallon jar of freshly made spaghetti sauce. The worker hit the refrigerator. The jar hit the floor and exploded. Glass and sauce flew in all directions. I ducked but I couldn't avoid the fallout. It splattered over my head and arms and dripped, warm and wet, down my face. No time to worry about that. Where was Cadillac?

There he was, crawling into a low, open cupboard. Leaping forward, I grabbed him by the hind leg. He struggled, but I held on and dragged him out. As I straightened up, my head banged the underside of a counter where a bag of flour was sitting near the edge. The jolt upset the flour, and it poured over Cadillac and me.

Dazed, coughing, half buried in white flour dust, I must have looked like a war victim caught in a snowstorm when I finally staggered out to the playground.

The first person I saw was the fire chief with a stopwatch in his hand. Then a flashbulb went off in my face. I stood there gaping, trying to get my bearings. All the classes in the school were lined up in neat rows, quietly waiting for the signal to go back to their rooms. I felt every eye on me.

Mom rushed up. For once she didn't try to teach me some lesson. She hustled Cadillac and me, dripping a trail of floured spaghetti sauce behind us, into her car and drove home.

11. Spaghetti Head

The next day was torture. The phone started ringing early. Two people called to say they wouldn't be able to distribute Mom's campaign literature in their neighborhoods. They had promised to do it, but something had come up. They were sorry.

This didn't seem to discourage Mom, probably because she was so busy getting the four of us organized to campaign at Lowell Park, where the sign-up for Little League would be going on all morning. I wanted Mom to go—I wouldn't be allowed to play baseball this season unless she went to pay the Little League fee, but I didn't want to go with her.

What had happened at school yesterday made me so embarrassed that I intended to spend the day at home with my head under a pillow. "Why do you have

70

to *campaign* at the park?" I demanded.

"Claude Wyman will be there all morning passing out his WHY NOT WYMAN? bumper stickers, so I have to be there, too. I can't let the voters think I'm not working as hard as he is or I'll never get elected."

Against my better judgment, I went to the park and stood at the entrance for an hour, shivering, holding an ETHEL BLODGETT FOR SCHOOL BOARD sign. It was taller than I was, so I hid behind it as much as I could. Olivia and Joel wandered all over the place, handing out cards with Mom's picture and a list of her qualifications.

Even Clarence Matthew did his share. He sat in his stroller wearing an enormous VOTE FOR BLODGETT pin. Mom stood in the sign-up line, chatting with everyone near her, smiling, laughing, having a great time.

I prayed no one I knew would come along. I hadn't been at the park more than ten minutes, though, before Jeff Higgins yelled, "Hey, Spaghetti Head, that's some picture of you in the paper today."

What picture? I didn't know what he was talking about, but I was afraid to ask. I tried to change the subject. "Did you see the game on TV last night? The Sox are going to win the pennant this year for sure."

"Got any meatballs to go with that spaghetti, Blodgett?" That was Toby, running up to join us.

I ignored him. "The Sox have got the best pitchers in the Eastern Division this season. You take—"

"You should have seen your expression when you came out of the kitchen yesterday with all that sauce on your head. Man, did you look funny!" Toby started to laugh, thinking about it.

"And that picture of him in the paper. Did you see it?" Jeff doubled up, he was laughing so hard.

Toby clapped his hand on Jeff's shoulder. Between haw-haws he spluttered, "I almost split my sides this morning when I spotted it. Right on the front page. There's Terry, holding his crazy pig, with spaghetti sauce dripping out of his hair."

I kept trying to act as if I didn't care. But I ended up yelling at them to go away and leave me alone.

Toby and Jeff were still snickering when they sauntered off. "You don't have to get mad, Spaghetti Head," Toby called back over his shoulder.

Mom finally relieved me of the sign. "I'll take over now, dear. You can go home, but take Olivia and Joel with you. I'd better stay at the park until the crowd leaves."

We took the long way home because I wanted to stop at the drugstore to get a newspaper. I didn't look at it, though, until I was safely in my room, alone, with the door shut.

The picture was even worse than I expected. It was directly under the center fold of the *Daily Sentinel* for everyone who lives in Brookside, Samoset, and Woodland to see. Hundreds, maybe thousands of people today were looking at that picture of me and giggling. How could I hold my head up again, ever?

Next to my picture was an article by Tom Reilly called, "School Fire Protection: Can It Be Improved?"

Five Brookside schools were listed, with the time it took to get all the children out of their buildings during a fire drill. The students at Longfellow were slower at leaving than any other school.

I was the one responsible for that time lag, I was sure of that. But I didn't see how I could rescue a pig and still get to the playground in record time. I felt like calling Tom Reilly and giving him a piece of my mind.

No sooner had I put down the paper than Mrs. Bush telephoned to say that she would not be able to give a coffee for Mom on Wednesday as she had planned. I had a suspicion that picture of me in the paper wasn't going to help Mom get elected to the School Board.

I told her that when she breezed in with Clarence Matthew at lunchtime, her cheeks pink from being out so long in the cool air.

"You may be right, Terry. But that picture could help me, too."

"Help? Are you kidding?"

Mom grabbed bologna, mayonnaise, and bread out of the refrigerator and starting putting sandwiches together. "Getting known. That's half the battle in getting elected. Some people will vote for anyone whose name they recognize."

Before we finished our sandwiches, another campaign worker called to say he wouldn't be able to hold Mom's sign at the polls on election day.

Mom brought out her lists of volunteers and crossed off the names. "We're shorthanded now. Don't make any plans for tomorrow, Terry. I'm going to need you all day to help me pass out my cards."

"I wanted to go down to the high school to practice baseball."

"You'll have to postpone your practice."

"I'm not going to spend all Sunday tramping around the streets of Brookside passing out dumb cards. Suppose someone sees me?"

"Someone should see you, Terry. That's the point."

"Can't you understand? Kids I know, kids from school. I can't bear to have them seeing me make a fool of myself again."

Mom smiled at me. "Campaigning for a good candidate, namely, your honest, dedicated, hard-working mother, is not making a fool of yourself."

I didn't see anything to smile about. "Everyone will laugh at me. How would you like to be called 'Piggy' and 'Spaghetti Head'? How would you like to have your picture in the paper showing you looking like an idiot?"

Mom stared at the lists in front of her and sighed. She looked tired. "Terry, all I can say is, I need you. I hope you'll come with us."

12. On the Campaign Trail

When Sunday came, I trooped out with the rest of the family. Twinky Rogers came with us, too. He was the only one of the gang on Pinecrest Drive who still played with us. The Foster twins, Christine, and Jimmy had been warned to stay away from the dirty Blodgetts.

None of us, except maybe Mom, was enthusiastic about tramping up to people's houses with campaign literature. Mom promised us treats at the Sundae Mundae Shop if we could cover Precinct 4. That gave us a little incentive.

We drove to Hancock Street, about three miles away from Pinecrest Drive, at the other end of Brookside. Mom parked the car and opened up a big map of the town. She drew a line with a Magic Marker around the outside edges of Precinct 4, then she divided the precinct into three parts. She would take Olivia and Clarence Matthew with her—they would cover one section of the precinct. Joel and Twinky would go together and take another section. The third part was my territory.

All we had to do was slip one of Mom's cards under each door and go on to the next house. That didn't sound too difficult. We would meet back at the car when we had finished.

I took my bundle of cards and started off. I walked fast down Hancock Street as if I were an old hand at campaigning. When I reached the corner of Hancock and Cedar Streets, where my area began, I was overwhelmed by shyness. How had I gotten into this? I felt like running away. Maybe I could bury the cards in the ground somewhere and pretend that I had delivered them. Mom would never know—she wouldn't have time to check up. Suppose she lost the election, though. How would I feel then?

I looked back up Hancock. Mom didn't just stuff her card in the door and go away—she rang each doorbell, waited for someone to answer, and introduced herself. She stood there, smiling, talking, looking as if meeting strange people was easy and pleasant.

Olivia was working the other side of the street. She didn't act shy, either, striding up to each door as if she owned the house. She would probably run for President someday.

I combed my hair back with my fingers. Olivia was not going to show me up. Get moving, I told myself.

When I turned off Hancock onto Cedar Street, I realized I'd never walked down that street before. The houses were old, with lots of large trees around them. Some of them were set far back from the street. I took a deep breath and marched up to number 3.

I felt like a burglar as I walked onto the open porch. A dog, sounding like a man-eater, started barking ferociously inside the house. Where could I put Mom's card so it wouldn't blow away?

There was no doormat, no storm door handle, nothing but the mail slot. Mom had made quite a point that campaign literature shouldn't be put in mailboxes, so I leaned down to slip the card under the door. Impossible. Metal weather stripping blocked off the space.

From inside I could hear the dog jumping and snarling. Could he get out? Probably he was locked in, but he made me nervous. I wanted to get rid of that card in a hurry, so I pushed it halfway through the mail slot. Instantly, the dog tore it out with his teeth. I didn't wait to find out what happened next.

Number 7. A red-haired man in baggy pants was washing his car in the driveway. I cleared my throat, handed Mom's card to him, muttered something about voting for Ethel Blodgett, and started to walk away.

"Hey, wait a minute, sonny. This Ethel Blodgett, she any relation to that pig woman Blodgett?"

"Ethel Blodgett is my mother." I hated hearing her referred to as "that pig woman."

"Some sort of pig freak is she? My neighbor was telling me about her. Keeps a load of pigs back of her house. They get out and run up and down the street making a pigpen of the whole neighborhood. You her boy?"

I felt mad all over, so mad I forgot to feel shy. "I'm her son and we don't have a 'load of pigs.' We have *one* pig and we're keeping it for only a little while." I held one finger up to make sure he focused on that number.

"She running for something?"

"School Board. And you should vote for her. She's a good person." I was surprised how loud my voice sounded.

The man stared at the card I had given him. "Yeah, well I guess we don't need any pigs on the School Board."

I didn't trust myself to say anything more—I was too furious. *I guess we don't need any pigs on the School Board.* How dare he talk that way about my mother! Was everyone in town calling Mom "that pig woman"?

Energy shot through me. Bury Mom's cards? Not a chance. I was going to deliver every one of them. I'd throw my shoulders back, look proud, walk up to every door, talk to everyone I met, shake hands, smile. No one in Precinct 4 was going to think the Blodgetts were crazy, dirty people. Not if I could help it. Pig woman! Who did that redheaded guy think he was?

At the next house an old lady opened the door, with the chain lock still fastened, and peered at me through the crack. She must have heard me coming. "Oh no, dear. I don't want any," she said as I came closer to her.

"It's for my mother, she's running for School Board."

"That's nice. You run along now."

I pushed a card into her hand and left. As I walked away I heard her bolting the door. She would probably drop Mom's card into the wastepaper basket without looking at it.

Like a mailman I trudged up to each house, deposited my message, moved on to the next door. Up one side of the street, down the other, opening gates, climbing steps, noticing how some homes had shining brass door handles and freshly painted window boxes while others had peeling paint and porches cluttered with junk.

On Oak Hill Road I approached a woman just getting out of her car. "I hope you'll vote for my mother. She's running for School Board," I said, putting on a pleasant face, feeling that I was getting the hang of this campaigning business.

The woman waved away the card I tried to give her. "I don't vote. They're all a bunch of bums," she said and disappeared into a small, dark bungalow.

Pig woman, freak, bum what other nasty words would I hear? I didn't care what they said anymore. I was going to do my best for Mom.

Several houses farther down the street I was in the

process of shoving a card under a door when the door flew open. I felt like a fool.

A woman laughed. "Who are you working for?" she said. She was square, brown-haired, and wore a dark-green sweater that had seen better days.

"My mother. She's Ethel Blodgett. She's running for School Board." I braced myself for an attack, expecting the woman to tell me that anyone who owned a pig wasn't fit to run for office.

Then I noticed that the woman was really reading Mom's card. "Ethel's a good candidate. I've known her for years in the League. You can tell her she's got my vote."

"You bet I'll tell her." I walked down the street feeling as if I'd been given a thousand-dollar bill.

On Beech Lane, though, my luck turned sour again. A couple were out in their yard, seeding the lawn. They stopped their work to look at Mom's card. "Ethel Blodgett, I've heard about *her*. Remember, Ed, she's the one who raises pigs."

"I don't care what she raises, so long as it isn't taxes. What's her position on closing the Quincy School?"

I had to admit I didn't know.

"You better find out some of these things before you go around passing out literature."

Hurt, but still determined, I kept on. Since Mom rang every doorbell, she must be getting more flak than I was. How could she stand it?

By the time I turned off Beech Lane onto Elm Street, the sky had clouded over and a chill wind made me hunch down inside my jacket and turn the collar up.

As I walked up to 17 Elm Street, I realized with a sinking feeling in my stomach that I recognized the house. Here, of all places, I hoped no one would notice me.

13. "You're Being Pigheaded"

But someone did. Just the person I didn't want to see. Mr. Harley, wearing paint-stained overalls and carrying a ladder, came around the corner of the house just as I was going up the walk. Mr. Harley was my Little League coach last year. He knows a lot about baseball, and boy is he a stickler.

If practice is called for 5:30, you'd better be there at 5:30. If he tells you to take a lead, you'd better take a lead. If he spends time teaching you how to bunt, you'd better know how to bunt at the next game.

"Well, Terry Blodgett, how are you?" he said in a friendly voice.

"Fine, fine."

"What brings you here to Elm Street?"

I handed him one of Mom's cards. He put his ladder

down on the ground and read the card. Had he heard all the talk about the pig? Did he think that having a pig made us sloppy garbage eaters? Maybe having a pig would disqualify me from playing baseball.

"Ummmmmm," was all Mr. Harley said. Then he slipped Mom's card into his back pocket. "Planning to try out for Little League next Saturday?"

"I thought I would." I hoped he wouldn't bring up anything about putting more power into my swing. He was always after me about that.

He didn't have a chance. Carl, his son, who was also in Little League, bounded up to me. "We laughed ourselves silly over that picture of you in the *Sentinel*, Terry."

My face was burning up, my feet were aching from walking so far, and my hopes of being recognized as a ballplayer worthy of being elected captain of his team were shattered. I turned my back on the Harleys and walked away.

"See you at tryouts on Saturday," Carl yelled after me.

I didn't answer. I didn't look back. Tears were dangerously close to spilling down my face. No one was going to catch me blubbering in public, no matter what happened.

By the time I met Mom at the car on Hancock Street, I was more discouraged than I had ever been in my life. I was also frozen—the temperature must have dropped ten degrees since we had started out. My hands were icy. The sky was a dismal gray. It looked the way I felt.

Two steaming-hot cups of chocolate at the Sundae Mundae Shop thawed me out a little, but they didn't cheer me up. Why couldn't I have thought of some smart remark to throw at Carl Harley? Why couldn't I have been blessed with a mother who worked as a bookkeeper instead of running for public office?

That night, after the little kids were in bed, Mom sat down beside me on the couch in the family room. "Tell me what reactions you got from people, Terry."

I didn't say anything—I wanted to forget the whole horrible day.

"The rumors are wilder than I expected," Mom said. "Did I tell you that another coffee has been canceled?"

I couldn't help feeling sorry for her. "I met a woman who thought you were wonderful."

"What's her name?"

"I didn't ask."

"Didn't ask? Supporters are more valuable than rubies. Where does she live?"

I strained to remember. "Oak Hill Road, I think."

Mom jumped up and grabbed her Voters List. "Elm, Hancock, Oak Hill Road. Here we are. Do you remember the number?"

I felt like a rubber band that is being stretched too far. Something snapped inside me. "No, I don't remember and I don't want to remember it. I hate your campaign and I hate your pig. They've ruined my whole life."

Mom put down the Voters List and put her hand on my arm. "Terry, dear, I think that's a bit of an exaggeration."

"It's the way I feel!"

The telephone rang. From what Mom said when she answered, I could tell Miss Dowd was on the other end of the line with a new complaint. Mom was very polite. She even thanked Miss Dowd for calling. Thank goodness I hadn't answered. I would have told Miss Dowd to go to blazes and slammed the phone down so hard she would have been deaf for a week.

Mom made herself a cup of instant coffee before she came back into the family room. She stood in the middle of the room for a while, not saying anything, just stirring her coffee.

That call meant more trouble and I didn't want to hear about it. But after a few minutes curiosity got the better of me. "What did Miss Dowd have to say?"

"The neighbors have signed a petition protesting our pig. They're presenting it to the Board of Health tomorrow night."

"Take Cadillac back to the farm. That's all you have to do. You're being pigheaded."

I expected Mom would bawl me out for talking to her like that. I was too mad to care, though.

"You're right, Terry. I am pigheaded. I'll take our pig back, but I'll take him back on my own terms, in my own time."

"And never mind what happens to the rest of us?"

Mom looked at me, her dark-blue eyes penetrating and kindly at the same time. "Is Cadillac really dirty?"

"Not with Olivia giving him baths and the rest of us

cleaning his house and yard and hosing it down every day."

"Has he turned the neighborhood into a slum?"

"Of course not."

"Don't you see that if I get rid of Cadillac immediately, that is admitting I'm wrong when I know I'm not?"

"The election is only one week away. You've got to do something fast or you'll lose."

"I have no intention of losing the election if I can help it."

"How can you possibly win? You're losing workers faster than a tree loses leaves in a hurricane."

"At sea, Terry, if the captain of a ship can't avoid a hurricane, he heads straight into the middle of it."

Very dramatic. I could hear the swell of an orchestra in the distance. What Mom didn't understand, though, was that I wasn't interested in battling hurricanes. I just wanted to get through the next week without being laughed out of Longfellow School.

14. A New Trick for Cadillac

That night I dreamed I was in the middle of a big arena, packed with everyone from town. Pigs, dozens of them, were running all around me. I was expected to catch them and put them in their pens. But as soon as I caught one, it escaped. The audience was laughing, clapping hands, stamping feet, whistling, yelling, jeering.

When I woke up the next morning, I felt tireder than when I went to bed. The day, the week, stretched ahead of me like a jail sentence. What could I do to get out of this mess I was in?

All the way to school I saw in my mind that newspaper picture of me holding Cadillac, with my hair soaked with spaghetti sauce. The closer I got to school, the slower I walked. I wished I was Terry Blodgett the Not

Very Noticeable again. Never, ever, did I want to be noticed the way I was being noticed now.

My head drooped; my shoulders sagged. I ducked through a side door as the first bell rang, and ran up to my classroom without speaking to anyone. Someone had tacked the newspaper picture of me on the bulletin board. A little knot of gigglers was gathered around it. "See, Blodgett's busted his brains!" Jeff Higgins was saying loudly. For once, I was glad to have school start so that I could concentrate on English and Social Studies.

At lunchtime Mrs. Lambartini left the room first, leading the class into the hall and down to the cafetorium. I lingered at my desk until the last person had disappeared. Then I dashed to the bulletin board, ripped off my picture, and hastily stuffed it in my pocket.

"Hey, Spaghetti Head, coming to tryouts on Saturday?" Toby yelled after we had finished lunch and were on the playground.

"He'd better stay home or he'll drip sauce all over the playing field," Jeff said.

"Come on, let's practice double plays." I grabbed Toby, who had a glove and ball in his hand, and shoved him into position. "You be shortstop. Jeff, you play second and I'll play first." I'd show those jokers I was good for something besides catching pigs.

Jeff scooped up the ball, flipped it to Toby, who tagged second and threw it to me on first. I caught it as neatly as any major leaguer. I began to cheer up. We tried the play again.

But this time, just as the ball was headed toward me, some character screams, "Piggy! Want some garbage?" and hurls his orange peel at me.

If only I'd had the brains to ignore him. But I glanced over to see who it was. At that moment the ball smacked me on the cheek—smacked me so hard I couldn't think of anything for a minute except the pain.

"Spaghetti Head, you're supposed to catch the ball with your glove, not your face!"

I moved away, rubbing my cheek, defeated. If only I could go back to being a nobody—that quiet kid, what's his name? From the looks of things, though, I was doomed to being a somebody. Not a baseball star somebody, but a stupid somebody with spaghetti for brains and a pig for a pet.

When I got home from school I had a nasty swollen bruise on my cheek. The smell that greeted me when I walked into the kitchen almost made me forget how much my face hurt. The counters were jammed with cinnamon rolls, coffee rings, butterscotch buns, banana bread, muffins. Olivia was standing on a chair, greasing a pan. Clarence Matthew, sitting in his high chair, was busy picking the nuts out of his bun and dropping them on the floor.

"You planning to open a bakery?" I asked Mom as she opened the door to the oven and slid in a pan of pecan rolls.

Instead of answering my question she inquired about my cheek, inspected it, gave me an ice pack to hold over it for a while. Then she buttered a cinnamon roll for me. She was up to something, something I'd be expected to help with, no doubt.

"Everyone has canceled out on the coffees I had scheduled for this week," Mom said almost gaily, setting the timer for ten minutes.

"What are you doing, then? Baking for Claude Wyman's coffees?"

Mom laughed. "I can give myself a coffee, can't I?"

I chewed the cinnamon bun slowly on the side of my mouth that didn't hurt. "No one will come. Everyone thinks we're pig freaks."

"That's where you're wrong, dear. Ever hear of a thing called curiosity?"

"It killed the cat."

"It may help me win this election. Saturday we are having Open House. Ten till two. Coffee and goodies for everyone who wants to come."

My fighting spirit came back in a rush. "Everyone except Terry Blodgett. I have Little League tryouts Saturday, and nothing—I repeat, *nothing*—is going to stop me from going to them."

Mom didn't argue. She didn't yell. She didn't even raise her voice. "Maybe you can help when you get home from tryouts. By the way, I have invitations that need to be delivered. On your way to the library you can drop them off at the houses on Washington Avenue."

"I wasn't planning to go to the library today."

Joel breezed in, scooped up a roll or three.

"You and Joel can distribute them together," Mom said calmly, as she started scrubbing the dirty pans in the sink.

What do you do with a mother like that? Throw a tantrum? Not that day. I was too tired.

We delivered the invitations. When we came home again, we found Olivia in Cadillac's pen, dressed in her red tights and a red tutu, with a whistle in her mouth. She was holding a pink hoop in one hand and a piece of stale bread in the other.

The whistle blew. Cadillac ran forward, jumped through the hoop, and claimed his prize, the piece of bread and a hug from Olivia.

Joel immediately got into the act. " 'Livia, let me hold the hoop. See if we can get him to jump higher."

Before long the great animal trainers were putting Cadillac through a routine. He would jump through the hoop, run to Joel, who would send him running after a rolled-up newspaper. Cadillac picked the paper up in his mouth and dropped it at Olivia's feet.

Amazing how Joel and Olivia loved that pig. They didn't seem to care that the neighbors weren't speaking to us and that Twinky was the only one who would play with us anymore. I couldn't help watching Cadillac myself. He was more interesting than I liked to admit.

"Terry, Terry, Ter, I got a great idea. Let's teach Cadillac to play baseball."

"Are you crazy, Joel? We'll have Miss Dowd out here screeching at us in thirty seconds."

"We'll aim the ball low—very, very low. She'll never know."

The idea intrigued me. The more I thought about it, the better I liked it.

15. Candidates Night

With white spray paint and a yardstick, we marked off a miniature baseball diamond in Cadillac's yard. Home plate was directly in front of the pig's house. Next we organized our game.

Joel pitched and I batted. Cadillac was stationed in the outfield at the far end of the pen. Olivia was with him to keep him more or less in position. We forgot about trying to perfect our major-league techniques in order to train Cadillac. Joel wound up and threw me a low, gentle ball which I hit just hard enough to land it near Cadillac. The pig picked it up and carried it to Joel, who tagged me out.

At first I could get all the way around the little diamond before Cadillac got the ball back to Joel. But Cadillac improved—before long he returned the ball before I reached first base. He got four sugared dough-nut holes for that stunt.

I had to baby-sit that night while Mom attended the Board of Health meeting. The neighbors were present-ing their petition and Mom went to defend herself.

When she came back she announced that the Board had agreed to let her keep Cadillac for one more week if, at the end of that time, she would take him back to the farm for good. After all the trouble that pig had caused me I thought I'd be overjoyed to hear her say that. But I wasn't. We had had fun playing with Cadil-lac that afternoon. I had the strange feeling that I would miss him when he left.

I wouldn't miss being called "Piggy" or "Spaghetti Head," though. Maybe when the pig was gone those names would fade away. I hoped so. I was getting tired of the lip I got from Toby and Jeff. I tried to build an invisible rubber wall around myself so that the words bounced off and didn't hurt me. Sometimes that worked. Sometimes it didn't.

Every day that week we played baseball games in our yard after school. I'd elected myself captain of our Little Hog team. It wasn't real baseball, of course, but it was fun. Twinky, Joel, Olivia, and I took turns playing every position on our pigpen diamond. Cadillac was a permanent outfielder. I tried to think of a way we could teach him to bat and pitch. He was good at pushing the ball with his snout, but smart as he was, he couldn't stand on two legs and hold a ball or a bat in his hoof.

He could play hide-and-seek, though. Every day he

94

got better at it. We would take a break from baseball and hide things to see if Cadillac could find them. He had already mastered the finding of hidden food. Gradually, he learned to sniff out clothes that belonged to us: sneakers, hats, scarves.

At first we would tuck them somewhere out of sight, under a bush, behind a fallen branch. Then we buried them in the ground. Cadillac became very skillful at rooting them out. We made a big fuss over him whenever he did this, hugging him, scratching him, feeding him the most delicious things we could find.

Mom kept us supplied with food incentives, slightly burned muffins or buns that she didn't think were good enough to serve at.her Open House on Saturday. Cadillac gobbled them up and looked for more. More were always available, because Mom spent most of her time that week baking, until our freezer was jammed and so were the freezers of what friends we had left.

Mrs. Hansen didn't go back on Mom, and neither did Mrs. Rogers. They were the only neighbors who would have anything to do with us.

When Joel and I walked to school in the morning or came home in the afternoon we always said hi to people who happened to be outside working in their yards. They used to stop for a minute and ask us how school was going. But not now. They would keep on working, pretending they didn't hear us.

Even Mrs. Wilson's cat, Lily, seemed to be ignoring us. She didn't mew and rub against our legs the way she used to.

Every day Mom's half-page invitation to the Open House was printed in the *Daily Sentinel.* Claude Wyman's ads were larger. Some of them had long lists of people in town who supported him. Others read: "It takes a man with sense to save your tax dollars."

That one really bugged Mom. Every time she read it she said, "Claude thinks he can run the schools the same way he runs his plumbing supplies company. He'll probably think he's increasing the quality of education by getting the town to install new faucets in every school."

Mom didn't have any coffees to go to that week— everyone had canceled out on her. But Thursday night was Candidates Night, run by the League of Women Voters. I was sure Mom would want me to stay home and baby-sit for her, but Thursday afternoon she announced that Mrs. Hansen would be taking care of the kids.

"I need you to stand outside the door of the auditorium, passing out my cards."

"I have homework."

"Get it done this afternoon. We don't have to arrive until seven thirty."

Why argue? I'd already done so much campaigning that a little more wouldn't kill me. I didn't realize, though, what a big deal the Candidates Night was.

Mom never goes to the hairdresser's. But she went that day and she spent a long time putting on makeup and getting dressed. She insisted that I spiff up, too, in my white shirt, tie, and plaid jacket. I felt as stiff as a robot.

Just before we left, Mom made a hurried telephone call

to one of her few loyal workers. "We're leaving now . . . yes . . . Keep him backstage . . . I'll come and get him."

What was she talking about? An uneasy feeling came over me.

When we reached the high school the parking lot already had lots of cars in it, and a steady stream of people was pouring into the building. I positioned myself outside near the entrance and handed one of Mom's cards to everyone who would take it.

At eight, when the program was scheduled to begin, I went inside. The auditorium seemed bright as I came in from the dark. Noisy, too. People stood in clusters discussing the candidates. Some of them walked up and down the aisles looking for a place to sit, nodding and waving to friends or stopping to chat. No one could say the voters weren't interested in this election —all the seats were filled.

I stood with the latecomers at the back of the hall, fidgeting with my tie, afraid that Claude Wyman would somehow make a fool of Mom.

The President of the League called the meeting to order. The candidates for selectmen filed up onto the stage. The three of them sat behind a long table, with glasses of water in front of them. One by one they came to the lectern to speak.

Forty-five boring minutes later they left the stage. Mom and Claude Wyman replaced them. Mr. Wyman was first. He put on his horn-rimmed glasses and read his talk. It was full of figures and percentages and was as dry as crackers.

When he sat down, the man standing next to me leaned over to a friend and whispered, "Wyman's got it sewed up." The friend nodded.

My heart was pounding and the palms of my hands were sweaty. I could hear the click of Mom's high heels as she came forward to the lectern. She looked pretty in her dark-blue dress.

Mom didn't have any notes. Resting her hands lightly on the sides of the lectern, she looked out at the audience and smiled, that warm friendly smile of hers, like the sun coming out after a storm. Tears welled up in my eyes—I wasn't sure why.

"Running for the School Board has been an educational experience for me," Mom began. "It has taught me how much the voters of Brookside care about who represents them. I, too, as a former teacher and now the mother of four children, care very deeply about the quality of education in our schools.

"Unfortunately, this campaign has also taught me how quickly rumors spread, and how, as they spread, they grow distorted out of all proportion to the original kernel of truth that started them. I'm going to pause here for a moment to bring out a visual aid."

Mom walked to the far side of the stage and reached for something behind the curtain.

What was she up to? No one in the audience coughed. Not one Voters Guide rustled. Every eye was on the stage.

As she walked back to the lectern, Mom carried a black case in her hand. Oh no! Not Cadillac!

16. The Open House

Mom put the black case on the floor beside her. "Talk has been circulating about how I keep dozens of huge, dirty pigs in my backyard at 37 Pinecrest Drive. I'd like to show you what started that talk."

The auditorium was so quiet you could have heard an ant crawling up the wall. Mom opened up the case and brought out our little pink-and-white pig. She held Cadillac in her arms as she walked, smiling, from one end of the stage to the other.

The audience burst out laughing. And then they clapped and whistled and laughed some more. Mom stepped up to the lectern again, still holding the pig. "This pig, no bigger than a large bag of flour, is the only pig I have ever had. It's the only pig I ever intend to have. I brought him to my home to show my children firsthand what a real farm animal is like. We have had him for about ten days and in less than a week we will take him back to the farm where he was born."

She put Cadillac in the animal carrying case and sent him backstage to another round of applause.

When the audience quieted, Mom's voice rose strong and clear. "What has all this to do with my running for the School Board?" She paused. "A great deal. You, as voters, have learned by this incident how I will react as your elected representative.

"You have learned that I do not collapse under pressure. You have learned that I will fight for what I consider educationally sound for your children and mine and that I have the courage to take risks, even at some cost to myself.

"I have demonstrated to you that I am not afraid to stand alone for my convictions, neither am I afraid to go along with the majority when I feel it is acting responsibly."

A thrill went through me—my mother was certainly the smartest woman in Brookside. When she sat down, she was given a big hand.

Now the questions began. Some guy in the audience asked Mom if she was planning to get a pig for every school as part of a back-to-nature movement.

Mom replied, "Of course not. But don't you think that allowing children to observe the real world is sound education? A picture is worth a thousand words, but a real experience is worth a thousand pictures."

From the back of the hall a woman with a shrill voice said, "I understand, Mrs. Blodgett, that when you took your pet to Longfellow School the pig disrupted the fire drill, which the fire chief was trying to conduct, so all the children weren't able to get out of the building quickly. Don't you think you could have come to the school at a better time?"

"What good is a fire drill if it occurs when you expect it or when nothing unusual is going on?" Mom asked her. "Fire drills ought to be tests of how well children and adults can react to unexpected circumstances."

I crossed my fingers on both hands, hoping Mom wouldn't run out of good, fast answers to the nasty questions. Miss Dowd sat stony-faced, three rows in front of me. The woman next to her wanted to know if Mom thought that children should learn to respect the property of others. Ouch.

Mom didn't blink. "Certainly we should all respect our neighbors' rights. That's why I didn't bring into my neighborhood, even for a short while, an animal that would keep people awake at night or molest the children."

When the meeting broke up I stood outside the door again, giving out Mom's cards.

"You've got to hand it to Ethel Blodgett," one lady said. "She's a good speaker."

"It takes more than being a good speaker to win elections," the man with her replied.

Mom knew she hadn't won the election yet. The minute Joel and I got home from school on Friday she put us to work.

We were assigned to yard detail. The grass wasn't long enough to be mowed, but we raked up every leaf and broken stick. Then we spread a thick layer of peat moss all around our red and yellow tulips so they looked even more beautiful than they were already. We scrubbed the toolshed. We scrubbed Cadillac's food dish and water pan. When we had finished our work, the yard was as neat as a golf course.

We tacked Ethel Blodgett posters all over the inside of our fence. We brought out long tables, which Mom had borrowed from the church, and set them up along one side of the yard. I was so busy I didn't get a single minute to sneak down to the high school diamond to practice baseball for the tryouts. All of us went to bed exhausted that night.

Early the next morning we gulped down just enough breakfast to keep us going, then set to work again. Dozens of balloons waited to be blown up and tied to the posts of our fence. We covered the long tables with red, white, and blue plastic which we weighted down at each corner with stones in case the wind came up. Then we trudged back and forth to the Rogers house and Mrs. Hansen's house carrying goodies from their freezers.

Gramp got a ride to our house with one of his friends so he could help pour the coffee. He arrived just as I left for the tryouts.

The high school field was crowded when I got there. I lined up according to the number I had been given when Mom signed me up. The sky was clear blue and the sun so warm that I didn't need a jacket. I'd been looking forward to this day for months and now it had finally come. It seemed perfect.

The wait in line lasted forever, half an hour at least. I couldn't figure out why, when I loved baseball more than anything in the world, I was anxious to get through and go home.

Finally I heard my number over the loudspeaker. I fielded some fly balls and some ground balls. Then I got into another slow-moving line to wait for a chance to bat.

"Watch out, Piggy, we're going to slice you up and fry you for bacon," Toby yelled at me.

I gave him a look, but said nothing. Why couldn't he lay off this pig business? Couldn't he see it wasn't funny?

As I came up to bat, I looked over at the coaches standing on the side of the field, watching, taking notes. One of them was Mr. Harley. I could feel his eyes on me as I stood at the plate, waiting.

Then came the windup and the pitch. I slammed a hard liner to deep right field. After two more hits, I was told to field hits made by other players. Then it was over. I could leave.

What had the coaches written down about me? Could they see that I'd be a valuable player on any team? Would the other players forget that my mother was "the pig woman" and vote for me as captain?

More questions came into my mind as I biked quickly toward home. What if no one had come to Mom's Open House? What if we had gone to all that trouble for nothing? I slowed down, dreading what I'd discover at Pinecrest Drive.

I needn't have worried, though. I could hardly make my way up the street because of all the cars parked on both sides. Our yard was jammed with people. Tom Reilly was one of them, his camera equipment slung over his shoulder. Mom, in a new green pants suit, strolled through the crowd, introducing herself, making sure she spoke to everyone. Clarence Matthew sat in his stroller near the kitchen door, wearing his VOTE FOR BLODGETT pin, eating buns, da-da-da'ing to himself, smiling whenever anyone spoke to him, proudly showing off his new upper tooth.

I filled a paper cup half full of cream, favored it with three teaspoons of sugar and a dash of coffee, and drank it in one gulp. Then I wolfed down three pecan rolls. Mrs. Rogers and Mrs. Hansen were flying back and forth between the tables and the kitchen keeping a steady supply of food available. I hoped Mom would get a vote for every compliment I heard about her food.

"Have you tasted those banana buns?"

"Mmmmmmmm. Marvelous. Try an oatmeal stick. They're out of this world." And the speakers would move off, munching happily.

Everyone in Brookside seemed to be in our yard. I

squeezed my way to Cadillac's pen, and there was Olivia in her red tutu, with circles of red rouge on her cheeks, holding her hoop, putting Cadillac through his tricks. She had tied an enormous red satin ribbon around his middle. Trouble was, it kept slipping around so that the bow was under his belly instead of on his back. Then it slipped off altogether.

Every few minutes Olivia would give Cadillac a rest. Then she would sit next to him, "reading" from her Mother Goose book. People stood by the fence, drinking their coffee, eating cakes, watching the show.

"I never knew pigs were so cute."

"Has your pig learned to read yet?" a lady called to Olivia.

"He's learning his sounds," Olivia replied solemnly.

Everyone laughed, including me. Then I looked over toward the gate and there, coming into the yard, was Mr. Harley. Right behind him was Miss Dowd. The laugh froze in my throat.

17. "Make the Lumber Talk!"

What I didn't see was Kaiser. I wondered about him, but I figured Miss Dowd had him tied up in her backyard. All thoughts of Kaiser, though, disappeared when I heard someone near me say, "Will you look at that? There's a baseball diamond painted in the pig's yard."

"Is your pig a left-handed batter or a right-handed batter?" a man asked Olivia.

"He's a catcher," she said, throwing a ball. Cadillac ran after it and brought it back to her.

Joel is almost as much of a show-off as Olivia. "You want to see him really play baseball?" he asked.

"A pig that plays baseball? What a riot!"

"Maybe Babe Ruth has been reincarnated as a pig!" Everyone chuckled.

Joel was inside the pen now, standing "on the

106

mound," holding the bat out to me. "Come on, Ter, let's have a game."

"Yay! Let's have a game. Yay!" The crowd around the fence looked at me and clapped.

I felt like an idiot. If I got into the pen, in front of all these people, everyone in Brookside would call me "Piggy." What if Mr. Harley saw me?

"Come on, Terry. Cadillac is awfully unpatient," Olivia said.

"Come on, Terry," the crowd echoed.

"Yeah, Ter, you bat and I'll pitch," Joel urged.

This was dumb, stupid, childish. I didn't mind playing games with the pig when just the family was around. But in front of the whole town?

"Come on, Terry," everyone chorused.

Against my better judgment, I allowed myself to be pushed into the pen.

My face and neck were burning up. I grabbed the bat. Joel spit on the ground and threw himself into his windup. I caught a glimpse of Miss Dowd, over by the coffee table, holding a paper cup of coffee. Then I saw Mr. Harley edging toward Cadillac's yard. I couldn't really be in this ridiculous situation. I must be having a nightmare.

Joel almost twisted himself into a figure eight with his windup. I hit a high fly ball. It moved out toward center field where Cadillac was waiting. The pig caught the ball in his mouth before it hit the ground. The crowd cheered and yelled, "One out."

Joel threw again. Low ball. I hit. The ball rolled along

the ground while I ran to first, to second. But I didn't make a run; Cadillac brought the ball to Joel who tagged me out before I reached third.

The spectators yelled, "Two outs."

Mr. Harley was standing near the fence now, watching intently. What was he thinking? That I was a jerk who shouldn't be allowed to play in Little League?

The crowd around the pen was bigger now. Two thirds of the people in the yard were watching us. The other third hovered around the food tables where Gramp had just set down a huge urn of freshly made coffee.

It was then that I noticed Kaiser for the first time. He was sitting at one end of the coffee table, slightly behind it. Miss Dowd had a leash on him and she was holding it loosely in one hand. With the other she was fiddling with her cameo. Mrs. Hansen was talking with her.

I was so busy thinking about Miss Dowd and Kaiser that I didn't watch Joel carefully enough as he pitched again. I swung and missed.

"Strike one," the crowd yelled.

"You going to let that runt of a pig get you out, Terry Blodgett?" That was Carl Harley, standing beside his father. Little twerp, who did he think he was?

A ball came toward me, very low, but I thought I could hit it. Another swing. Another miss.

"Strike two."

I was edgy now. This make-believe game on a miniature diamond had suddenly become a big deal. What had started as a trick to show off how smart Cadillac was had become a demonstration of how stupid I was. It was a contest now. Me against the pig. I was darned if I was going to lose my reputation as a good baseball player to a pork chop.

"Go, Terry, go. Go, Terry, go," chanted Twinky. The crowd picked it up. "Go, Terry, go. Go, Terry, go."

Over on the rise of ground by the back door, my baby brother sat quietly in his stroller. Someone had tied a balloon to it and Clarence Matthew was batting the balloon with his hand, watching it pop back to him. Mrs. Wilson's white cat, Lily, had sneaked into the yard and was sitting in front of the stroller watching the balloon, too.

I looked back at Joel winding up for another pitch. "Make the lumber talk!" someone yelled at me. The crowd hushed and pressed forward to catch the action. All those staring eyes were not going to see me strike out. I'd hit that ball if it was the last thing I did.

Joel's pitch came, high and fast. I socked it so that it sailed over Cadillac's fence, over the heads of the spectators, missed Clarence Matthew by a hair, and whomped Lily the cat just as she touched the balloon with her claws.

The cat yowled, the balloon exploded, the baby howled, and Kaiser shot forward.

"Look out for the coffee!"

18. Cadillac to the Rescue

Kaiser hit the table, so that it rocked forward. The huge urn toppled, hurling coffee grounds and scalding coffee before it. Trays of buns and cakes slid onto the ground. Screaming, yelling, screeching, the crowd scrambled to avoid the torrent.

The terrified cat raced for our maple tree, with Kaiser, barking furiously, charging after her. Straight through the middle of the crowd they ran, a path opening up before them as people jumped out of their way. Nobody was hurting Cadillac, but the commotion set him to squealing fit to split your ear drums. Joel grabbed and held him for dear life, while Olivia and I stood close by trying to soothe and calm him.

Everyone forgot about the baseball game, forgot about Ethel Blodgett's coffee party. All anyone wanted now was to get away from the hubbub without being trampled. Except Tom Reilly. He was calmly snapping pictures right and left in an attempt to preserve our disaster for the pages of the *Daily Sentinel.*

Children wailed while their parents pushed or pulled or carried them toward the street, proper good-bys and thank yous forgotten in the confusion. Lily was high up in the maple tree now, meowing, while Kaiser jumped and yelped at her from below.

The yard looked as if a tornado had struck. Mom's magnificent buns had been mashed to crumbs on the ground. Paper plates, napkins, and cups were everywhere. The big silver-colored coffee urn lay on the ground like a dead knight.

Holding a sobbing Clarence Matthew in her arms, Mom marched up to Miss Dowd. "Take that dog and get out of here!" Sparks almost jumped out of her eyes. I'd never heard her talk like that before.

"Those boys were playing baseball. You told me you wouldn't allow them to play in the yard any more. That big hard baseball, it's enough to . ."

"Take that dog home. Please."

Miss Dowd picked up the leash dangling from Kaiser's collar and, after a struggle, managed to get him out of the yard. Gramp pushed the gate shut behind them. "What are we going to do about Lily, Ethel?"

"I don't care about Lily," Mom said, her voice was flat as an old tire. She sat down on the back steps, hugging Clarence Matthew to her, looking as if she wanted to cry, too.

I went to her and put my hand on her shoulder. "Oh, Mom, Mom."

She didn't say anything for a long time. Then she patted my hand. "It's all right, Terry."

Gramp, Mrs. Hansen, and Mrs. Rogers moved quietly around the yard, picking up the mess. I helped, too. Might as well. Nothing else to do. No one said much. We all felt as if we had had the wind knocked out of us.

A squashed cinnamon bun lay beside a yellow tulip. I picked it up and fed it to Cadillac. It seemed to make him feel better.

Mom put Clarence Matthew in his crib for a nap. Then she drove Gramp back to his apartment, taking Olivia with her. Mrs. Rogers and Mrs. Hansen went home. Joel went off to play with Twinky. Just a little while before, our yard had been mobbed. Now I was the only one left, except for the pig. I felt a heavy stillness around me.

I let Cadillac loose in the yard—he was the best way of cleaning up the stray bread scraps. He trotted around sampling a bit of coffee cake here, a piece of frosted bun there, curling and uncurling his tail, making deep-throated pleasure sounds.

As I sat on the back steps watching him, I tried to figure out if either Mom or I could save anything from the rubble of the last two weeks.

All of a sudden I felt someone's presence. When I got up to look around I saw Miss Dowd, her brown speckled hand holding on to one of the gateposts.

"You have everything almost cleaned up," she said.

That old witch—how dare she come around to spy! I felt like telling her to fly away on her broomstick.

Her hand flew up to her neck and I noticed that the cameo she always wore wasn't there. "My cameo. It's gone," she said.

"I didn't steal it and the pig didn't eat it," I yelled at her.

"The ribbon was worn. I should have bought a new one, but it was Mother's. I liked wearing it just the way she did."

She looked so pathetic I began to feel sorry for her. After all the trouble she had caused us, I should have told her to clear out. Instead I opened the gate for her. "You want to come in and look for it?"

Miss Dowd walked past me as if I weren't there and started to peer around. I closed the gate, picked up Cadillac to put him back in his pen, and then I stopped. A light bulb came on in my head. "Our pig can help you find your necklace."

She paid no attention to me. "Someone must have stamped it into the ground."

I didn't give up. "Did you know that a pig's nose is more sensitive than a dog's?"

Miss Dowd sniffed as if her nose had caught a whiff of skunk. "Mother gave it to me just a week before she died. I've worn it ever since. I don't feel properly dressed without it."

"Would you really like to find it?"

"Of course I'd like to find it. What do you think I came over here for?"

I'd like to have given her an earful but I kept my temper. "Our pig can help you."

Miss Dowd turned her back on me and stooped to look under one of the tables.

"Do you have a handkerchief?"

She straightened up and threw me a cold stare. "Don't you have a handkerchief of your own you can use?"

My patience was threadbare. "Let me have your handkerchief!"

She looked frightened, as if I were going to attack her. Slowly she pulled a lacy white handkerchief from her sleeve.

I held it up to Cadillac's nose so that he could sniff it. Then I put him down on the ground. "Go find the necklace, Cadillac."

He sniffed the dirt, zigzagging all over the yard. When he became distracted by a chunk of banana bread, I held the handkerchief to his nose again.

"Give me back my handkerchief."

I gave Cadillac one last sniff and handed it back. The pig circled around where the food had been. He began to root in a spot where the grass had been worn away and the soil chewed up by the shoes of half the population of Brookside. Very soon, Cadillac picked up a dirty ribbon in his mouth and brought it to me.

"Good pig, good pig." I rewarded him with a chunk

of banana bread. As I scratched behind his ears, I could have sworn he smiled up at me.

The ribbon was grimy but the cameo was still pinned securely to it. Miss Dowd touched it almost reverently when I placed it in her hand. "I wouldn't have thought it possible . . . a pig . . . well!"

Another light bulb flashed on. "Wait a minute. Don't move. Stay right there!" I flew into the house, grabbed the polaroid camera, and raced back. "Miss Dowd, hold the necklace up in front of you."

On my first try I got a perfect, clear picture. I was admiring it when Mom drove into the yard. I glanced at my watch. Not a second to lose. I put the picture in my shirt pocket, jumped on my bike, and yelled at Mom, "I'll be back."

"Terry Blodgett, where are you going?"

I grinned at her. "You'll see."

19. An Unexpected Reward

Mom and I had been in trouble ever since that pig came to our house. Cadillac had spoiled Mom's chance of being elected to the School Board and my chance of being elected captain of an AAA Little League team. True, he had made us famous overnight. But in the wrong way. Mom's supporters had deserted her, and mine had laughed me out of the competition. But now Cadillac might be able to undo some of the damage he had done.

I pedaled faster. Darn it, why was I hitting every red light when I was in such a hurry?

I braked to a stop in front of the *Sentinel* office just as the clock on the tower of Town Hall began to strike four. Taking the steps two at a time, I raced to the second floor and pulled open the door of the office.

"Tom Reilly—I've got to see Tom Reilly," I panted.

"You just missed him."

"I've got to see him. Right now. I can't wait."

"You might be able to catch him in the parking lot, if you hurry."

Tom was getting into his car when I reached the parking lot. I was so out of breath that I could hardly talk. "Wait. A story. I've got a story for you."

He slammed shut the door of his car, rolled down the window, and leaned out. "You okay, kid?"

"Yeah. I've got a story for you." I pulled out the polaroid picture showing Miss Dowd and her cameo and explained how Cadillac had sniffed out the lost necklace.

"H'mmmm," Tom said.

"H'mmmm? What do you mean 'h'mmmm'? You were all over our property today taking pictures. I'll bet you got some beauties of the coffee urn falling and people stampeding out of the yard. You'll have a very funny story in Monday's *Sentinel* about everything that went wrong. How about printing something that went *right?*" I couldn't believe that was Terry Blodgett talking.

"You're pretty upset about this whole thing, aren't you?"

That was the understatement of the century. "How would you like to be the laughingstock of the town because of what the paper prints about you?"

Tom smiled. "I guess you've got a point there. I'll see what I can do, but I'm not promising anything." He

117

took my picture, rolled up his window, and drove off.

I biked home slowly, feeling tired and let down. Wasn't anything going to work out right?

Sunday, the day before the election, was rainy and cold. The warm, springlike weather was gone. Winter had returned.

Dad telephoned from Dallas, while we were eating lunch, to say he would be home on Tuesday. I couldn't wait to see him—it seemed like two years instead of two weeks that he had been away.

In the afternoon Mom drove us out to do some last-minute campaigning. It was rough business in the wet, with the temperature close to freezing. We gave up before long and came home. Mom built a fire in the fireplace of the family room. We popped corn and played Monopoly until bedtime.

Election day was as dark and cold and rainy as the day before had been.

"You're not going to hold up your 'ETHEL BLODGETT FOR SCHOOL BOARD' signs at the polls in this weather, are you, Mom?" I asked as I poured brown sugar on my bowl of Cream of Wheat.

"I suppose it is silly. Everyone has decided how to vote by this time, but I think I'll go through with it, anyway. The weather is supposed to clear."

She covered the sign with clear plastic and drove me to the Quincy School, where everyone in Precinct 4 votes. I stood on the sidewalk in the early-morning grayness, wearing my yellow slicker and high black boots, holding an umbrella in one hand and the sign in the other, while the rain fell in a steady drip, drip, drip, and the cold numbed my hands through my mittens

A Claude Wyman supporter was out, too, holding his sign several feet away from me. Fortunately he didn't make any move to speak to me—I was too miserable to say a word. The minutes of my hour of duty dragged by.

When Mom drove by to pick me up, I jumped into the car before she came to a full stop. "I never want to hear the word 'campaign' again as long as I live," I told her, flinging the sign into the backseat. Mom parked the car and handed me a thermos full of hot cocoa and a jelly doughnut. That cheered me up a little.

In a few minutes Mom steered the car away from the curb and headed toward Longfellow School. I ate the doughnut slowly while I listened to the sound of the tires on the wet pavement and the windshield wipers slapping back and forth.

"How are the Red Sox doing this season, Terry?"

"Huh?"

"The Red Sox. Will they win the pennant this year?"

The rain must have affected my hearing; my mother, the great baseball hater, wasn't interested in the Red Sox.

"I've been thinking," Mom continued. "You've done so much to help me these last weeks. Whether I win or lose, you deserve a special reward."

I emptied the last drops of cocoa from the thermos and wondered what she was hinting at.

"What would you think about my taking you to a couple of games at Fenway Park this summer?"

"Mom, you must be kidding."

"I'm serious. I've never been to a major-league baseball game. It will be an educational experience for me. It's about time I started attending your Little League games, too. You've been through a lot on my account, Terry. I can certainly do this for you."

Wow! Things were looking up. I floated into school in a daze, with a smile on my face so wide you could tie it in a bow at the back of my head.

"Hey, Piggy, hear you had a ruckus at your house Saturday," Toby said as I came into our classroom.

"Yeah, Spaghetti Head, people were throwing boiling coffee at each other and food was flying all over the place," Jeff added.

I looked at the two of them and grinned. "Yeah, you guys missed all the fun. It was the most exciting show Brookside ever had. How come you weren't there? The best part happened after everyone went home."

"What do you mean by that?"

"Just wait until you see the *Sentinel* today. You'll read all about it in there." I gave them a knowing look and took my seat just as the last bell rang.

When my head was buried in my social studies book, I began to have second thoughts about what I'd said. Tom Reilly might let me down. The *Sentinel* could print a picture of me looking foolish during the Open House fiasco. What would I do then?

By the time school was dismissed, the air had leaked

out of my confidence. I ducked into the drugstore to pick up a paper on my way home. But the *Sentinel* was sold out.

All afternoon I stayed inside the house, afraid to show my face. Olivia didn't help much. She cried for hours because Mom had taken Cadillac back to the farm. Even though Mr. Roscoe had told her she could come to see the pig as often as she liked, she acted as if we'd had a death in the family.

Late in the day the rain stopped. I looked out at the backyard to see the sun shining golden on the toolshed. Rakes and lawn mowers would be living there from now on instead of our pink-and-white pig. Why did I feel a lump in my throat?

20. Election Results

I was so sure the *Sentinel* had published something that made me look ridiculous that I didn't even ask Mom about it. Anyway, she looked exhausted when she came in from taking the last hour of sign-holding at Quincy School.

Gramp, Mrs. Rogers, and Mrs. Hansen gathered in the family room to wait with us for the election returns. Clarence Matthew was put to bed, but Joel and I and Olivia were allowed to stay up. The town had voting machines—we wouldn't have to wait too long.

Joel attached balloons, left over from the Open House, to the antlers of the moose head. None of us felt very cheerful, though. Mom drank two cups of black coffee.

At last the phone rang. Results from Precinct 1 were

in. Claude Wyman had won it.

"But only by 36 votes," Mom said, as she carefully printed the figures on a chart she had taped on the wall next to the phone.

We all sat gloomily waiting for the phone to ring again. When it did, hope glimmered. Mom had won in Precinct 3, but lost in 6.

Olivia huddled close to Mom on the sofa, clutching her stuffed monkey. Joel sat on the floor building a rocket with Legos. I busied myself making the control center to go with it, anything to keep myself busy. The suspense was agony.

Precinct 2—a win for Mom, but a narrow one. Mom and Mr. Wyman had each won two precincts now. However, Mr. Wyman's total count was ahead by 28 votes.

"It's going to be a squeaker, Ethel," Gramp said, stirring sugar into his coffee.

Mom won Precinct 8 and that gave her a lead. That's the precinct we live in. Winning it meant a lot to Mom. She brought a cherry cheesecake out of the refrigerator, sliced pieces for all of us and handed them around. "You see, Amelia's talk didn't turn everyone against me after all." Her face was bright with pride.

Only three more precincts to hear from. Joel's rocket was half built. It was red, white, and blue, and it would be huge when he finished it. I put the roof on the control center.

Claude Wyman took the lead away from Mom by winning in Precinct 7. Now Mom trailed by 19 votes.

Precincts 4 and 5 were the only ones left to hear from. The phone rang again. Mom answered in a calm, cool voice. "No, we don't chew Chunky Chocks. No, we're not interested in receiving a free sample," she said, and hung up.

"At ten at night wouldn't you think those sales reps would call it a day?" Mrs. Rogers said.

"The girl was taking a survey. She said I had been especially chosen to give my opinion." Mom laughed. She seemed to be feeling optimistic. I couldn't figure out why, though.

The doorbell rang. I jumped up to answer it, anxious to have some way of using all the nervous energy I was generating. Who was calling at this hour of the night? Tom Reilly.

"How'd you like that story I wrote about your pig in the *Sentinel*?" he asked me, as he stepped into the hall.

"What story?"

"You mean you haven't seen it?"

"Nice to have you here, Tom," Mom said in her warm, hospitable way. "Come join us in the family room. We've been saving a piece of cherry cheesecake for you."

Tom pulled a copy of the *Sentinel* out of his back pocket, opened it to page 3 and spread it on the coffee table in front of us. "That bank robbery in Samoset pushed you off the front page, but I did the best I could by you." All of us circled round the table to see the article. I hardly dared look but when I did I was happily surprised by what I saw.

124

Under the headline "Pig Finds Heirloom" was a big picture of Miss Dowd and her cameo. Tom hadn't used my picture—he had taken his own when he went to interview Miss Dowd. He had even quoted her as saying that she was grateful to Cadillac for finding her necklace. There were no pictures of the Blodgetts looking ridiculous at the Open House. In fact, there was very little mention of the Open House, only enough to explain how the cameo had been lost.

I could feel hope stirring inside me. Joel snapped together the final parts of the nose cone for his rocket. The phone rang.

The Precinct 5 figures were in. Mom won there, but just barely. She still trailed Wyman by 10 votes. The election hung on the results from Precinct 4.

I thought of the day we had campaigned in that area: the house where the dog tore up Mom's card, the man who had said we didn't need any pigs on the School Board, the old lady who had left the chain lock on her door while she talked to me, the woman who had said everyone who ran for office was a bum, the woman who said Mom was a good candidate, the man who was worried about his taxes being raised, and, last of all, Mr. Harley. How many of these people had voted? How many had voted for Mom?

"Are you conceding, Mrs. Blodgett?" Tom asked with a smile.

"Of course I'm not conceding. Have another cup of coffee and hang around for a bit so you can cover my victory celebration."

The phone rang again. We all jumped. Silently, we watched Mom stride briskly to the end of the room to pick it up. Miss Dowd was calling to ask how the election had turned out.

"She's got some nerve asking that," I said.

"Oh, Terry, that's her way of apologizing for all the trouble she's caused."

We bunched together in the center of the room, not saying much, waiting. Joel set his rocket on a launching pad ready for lift-off. Minutes ticked by.

The jangling of the telephone ripped the quiet. Had Mom won?

She held the receiver toward me and said, "For you, Terry."

For me? Who would be calling *me*? Mr. Harley was calling.

"You're too good a player for AAA," he said. "We'd like you in the Majors this year. I'll be coaching. Glad to have you aboard."

Majors! I hadn't even tried to make the Majors! I didn't care now whether I was elected captain of the team or not. I repeated those beautiful words over and over: *You're too good a player for AAA.* The initials N.V.N. didn't apply to me now, and I was going to be noticeable in a way I liked. Even if Toby and Jeff still called me "Piggy," I'd be "Piggy who played in Majors."

The Precinct 4 results came at last. The final precinct. Mom had won it. Not big. But she won it. She had been elected the new member of Brookside's

School Board by a margin of 23 votes.

"Blast off!" Joel yelled, and sent his beautiful red-white-and-blue rocket zooming up toward the ceiling.

I hugged Mom, she hugged me, and soon we were all hugging, laughing, crying with relief, patting each other's backs, the room one joyous scene of triumph.

"I've got to call Harvey in Dallas!" Mom exclaimed, rushing to the phone, dialing with quick, energetic strokes.

I stood in the center of the room, grinning. *Too good for AAA,* I thought again.

Then I wound up and hurled an imaginary ball that was so straight, so strong, yet so unexpected that the best batter in the world would have struck out. And even Cadillac would have had trouble catching it.

ABOUT THE AUTHOR

Susan Fleming is a free-lance writer who used to be a teacher and editor. Reading and the teaching of reading have been a special part of her life. She lives with her husband and two children in Massachusetts. This is her second book.